rough fascination

A HARMLESS WORLD NOVEL

ROUGH 'N READY
BOOK TWO

MELISSA SCHROEDER

EDITED BY
CHLOE VALE

COVER ART BY
SCOTT CARPENTER

HARMLESS PUBLISHING

contents

also by melissa schroeder

THE HARMLESS WORLD

The Original Harmless Five

- A Little Harmless Sex
- A Little Harmless Pleasure
- A Little Harmless Obsession
- A Little Harmless Lie
- A Little Harmless Addiction

Rough 'n Ready

- Rough Submission
- Rough Fascination
- Rough Fantasy
- Rough Ride

Harmless Trouble

- Harmless Secrets
- Harmless Revenge
- Harmless Scandals

The Wulf Family

- Faith

- Taboo
- Trust

A Little Harmless Military Romance

- Infatuation
- Possession
- Surrender

Task Force Hawaii

- Seductive Reasoning
- Hostile Desires
- Constant Craving
- Tangled Passions
- Wicked Temptations
- Twisted Emotions-coming 2025

The Camos and Cupcakes World

Camos and Cupcakes

- Delicious
- Luscious
- Scrumptious

The Fillmore Siblings

- Hate to Love You

- Love to Hate You

Juniper Springs

- Wild Love
- Crazy Love
- Last Love
- Imperfect Love

THE SANTINI WORLD

The Santinis

- Leonardo
- Marco
- Gianni
- Vicente
- A Santini Christmas
- A Santini in Love
- Falling for a Santini
- One Night with a Santini
- A Santini Takes the Fall
- A Santini's Heart
- Loving a Santini

Semper Fi Marines

- Tease Me
- Tempt Me

- Touch Me

- Falling for the Girl Next Door
- Falling for my Best Friend
- Falling for my Baby Mama

Also Included

- Kiss my Tinsel
- Dad Bod Rockstar

Texas Temptations

- Conquering India
- Delilah's Downfall

Hawaiian Holidays

- Mele Kalikimaka, Baby
- Sex on the Beach
- Getting Lei'd

Once Upon an Accident

- The Accidental Countess
- Lessons in Seduction
- The Spy Who Loved Her

The Cursed Clan

- Callum
- Angus
- Logan
- Fletcher
- Anice

The Sweet Shoppe

- Tempting Prudence
- Cowboy Up
- Her Wicked Warrior

By Blood

- Desire by Blood
- Seduction by Blood

Hands On

- The Hired Hand
- Hands on Training

Telepathic Cravings

- Voices Carry
- Lost in Emotion
- Hard Habit to Break

Bounty Hunters, Inc

- For Love or Honor
- Sinner's Delight

Saints and Sinners

- Seducing the Saint
- Hunting Mila

Lonestar Wolf Pack

- Primal Instincts

Texas Heat

- Scorched

Spies, Lies, and Alibis

- The Boss

SINGLE TITLES

- A Calculated Seduction
- Chasing Luck
- Going for Eight
- Grace Under Pressure
- Operation Love
- Saving Thea
- Snowbound Seduction
- Sweet Patience
- The Last Detail
- The Seduction of Widow McEwan

hawaiian terms

Aloha - Hello, goodbye, love
Bra-Bro
Bruddah- brother, term of endearment
Haole-Newcomer to the islands
Howzit - How is it going?
Kamaʻāina-Local to the islands
Mahalo-Thank you
Malasadas- A Portuguese donut without a hole which started out as a tradition for Shrove (Fat) Tuesday. They are deep fried, dipped in sugar or cinnamon and sugar. In other words, it is a decadent treat every person must try when they go to Hawaii. If you do not try it, you fail. Do yourself a favor. Go to Leonard's and buy one. You are welcome.
Pupule - crazy
Slippahs - slippers, AKA sandals

dedication

To Brandy Walker for keeping me on schedule and for being so much fun during Harmless in Hawaii. Your love of the absurd always makes me laugh. To Ali Flores who has one of the kindest hearts and sweetest souls. One of these days, Joy and I will make you design a plan and stick to it. And to Joy Harris, who is always more than her name and understands what being a Cappy is all about. You truly are a friend of romance and to every romance author out there.

You three ladies make this crazy publishing world a little less crazy.

Thanks,

Mel

Maura Dillon pushed open the door to the ER as she shook off Zeke's hand. The smell of the hospital still had her head spinning. She hated it, hated the way it made her feel. She remembered sitting in a similar ER years ago, waiting for her brother to show up and knowing that her parents were dead. The smell of antiseptic still made her want to puke.

A large hand clamped down on her shoulder, and she shook it off.

"Don't fuck with me, Zeke."

She heard the exasperated sigh and ignored it. The only thing she gave a damn about was getting to Conner. Of course, Zeke just kept following her.

"Love, if you go in there screaming at him, it isn't going to help."

She stopped in her tracks, drew in a deep breath, and looked at him. "Being gentle and sweet hasn't worked."

He cocked an eyebrow. "You've been sweet?"

She rolled her eyes. "Have I bitched about him working

1

eighty hours a week? No, I just let it go. I saw how bad he looked, and I let it go. I suggested vacations, weekend trips, and taking a fucking day off. Did he listen to me? No. And now look what happened."

Without waiting for an answer, she turned on her heel and walked up to the attendant window.

A woman who looked to be in her forties was writing something down as slow as a turtle. Lord, her nerves were jumping beneath her skin. Her stomach was tied in knots. When the woman finally looked up at her, Maura said, "I'm here to see jackass Conner Dillon."

The woman's lips twitched. "I take it you're his sister?"

She nodded.

"He's in room four, second door on the left."

She hit a button and a buzz sounded. The doors swung open, and Maura hurried through them. Fear and anger churned in her gut. With each step, her anxiety increased. He was the only person she had left in the world. They had each other and that had been enough. When she'd gotten the call from the ER doctor, everything had stopped. She might not have many close friends, and her romantic relationships were embarrassingly few and far between, but she could not lose Conner. It just could not happen. When she reached the door, Zeke stopped her.

"Take a deep breath, Maura."

She closed her eyes and did just as Zeke ordered.

"The doctor told you he's going to be okay, so take it that way. If you go in there screaming like a banshee, he'll get even more stubborn."

She nodded and opened her eyes. "We're in agreement, right? He has to take a month off."

Zeke nodded. "Sure. I've got my mate Rory coming over to help us out. Conner is going on vacation."

"Whether he likes it or not."

How the fuck did I end up here?

It was the only thought that came to mind when Conner Dillon looked around the small quarters. It wasn't the fact that it was sparse in amenities that bothered him. He didn't like clutter. Actually, he liked the little apartment. It had a small kitchen and eating area, with a no-nonsense bathroom and bedroom. He had a big house in Miami, but this suited him just as fine. So his irritation wasn't about the living area—it was about the location. There was only one person in the world who could get him to Hawaii when they had a big job in LA to handle.

Maura.

It only took one freaking doctor telling her that Conner's chest pains were a sign that something was seriously wrong, and that Conner was heading toward a heart attack, for Maura to breakdown. After losing both of their parents when Maura was only a teenager, she had freaked. And this time, his best friend and business partner Zeke had turned on Conner and sided with Maura. *Bastard*. There had been no fighting the two of them.

Now he was in fucking Hawaii.

"Is there something wrong?" the sultry southern voice asked from behind him.

He turned and looked at his new landlady for the next month. Jillian Sawyer was a contradiction in terms. Her voice spoke of her upper-middle class upbringing in Atlanta. Whenever he heard her speak, he thought of hot summer nights and necking on the back porch. He'd been feeling uneasy since she'd opened the front door.

The tattoos down her arms and braided hair, along with the nose piercing, would be a shock to most people. The light cocoa skin brought out her sea green eyes, and she was graced with the most amazing bone structure. Most people wouldn't suspect she had one of the highest IQ's of her graduating college class— or so his sister had told him. Her dress didn't fit with her upbringing. A worn out T-shirt cupped her abundant breasts and stopped just above her pierce navel. Her jeans were just as worn, hung low on her hips, and clung to every damn curve.

She cleared her throat, and he realized that he had been staring at her for several moments without saying anything. He tried to ignore the way his blood was starting to heat and smiled at her.

"No. The space is good."

Her lips twitched. "Don't overwhelm me with your praise, Conner."

He hadn't missed the sarcastic tone, and he was pretty sure his sister had acquired it from her the two years they'd roomed together at the University of Georgia.

"Sorry. I just don't like mandatory vacations."

"From what your sister says, you don't like vacations at all."

He could tell she was fucking with him. There was always a

look in her eyes that warned she was in a mood. He should let it go because it would start out as flirting and end with them yelling at each other. But, right at this moment, he didn't want to. Something was urging him to tease her.

He opened his mouth to respond but her cell phone rang out the University of Georgia fight song.

"Speak of the devil," she said before answering. "Yes, your big brother is here, and he's fine. I understand the FBI taught him how to get around on planes. And, seeing that he's an old man, he knows how to drive. He made it all the way over here to my little oasis without getting lost or running anyone over."

She was silent for a moment or two, and Conner could just imagine his sister rattling off instructions.

"I'm sure it was very serious. Of course, bugging him constantly is going to end up being worse for him. He came here to rest, so you need to let him do it. Do you want to talk to him?" Silence again. "Okay, well you get some rest and behave."

She hung up and gave him a cocky smile.

"Your sister is concerned."

He rolled his eyes. "Tell me about it. I can't believe she talked me into coming here."

She shook her head. "What a shame. You have to spend time in Hawaii relaxing. Quit being such a whiner."

Before he could respond, there was a shout from outside.

"Jillian, love, what are you doing in there?"

"Give me a second."

She turned and headed toward the door. After flinging it open, she settled her hands on her hips.

"What do you want, Mick?"

"Adam and I are going for a ride. Wanna come with?"

She shook her head. "No, I have a new tenant to attend to. You two have a good ride."

She shut the door and turned to face him. She shoved her hands into the pockets of her jeans and tapped her thumbs against the fabric. "Well, what do you think?"

"I already said it was a good space." He noticed her fidget, and Jillian didn't do it that often. He didn't know much about the woman, but he did know this was a sure sign she was nervous. He didn't think he'd ever seen her nervous before. Not like this.

"Cool. I have some work to do, so if you can handle settling yourself in, I need to get back to it."

He cocked his head to the side and studied her. He had known her, or known of her, for about ten years, but he realized then how little he knew about her.

"You just told your friend you couldn't go for a ride because you would be helping me."

Her cheeks reddened. "I don't like lying, but I have a deadline breathing down my neck. Mick and Adam don't understand about that. They think being a writer is just all fun and games."

"Isn't it?"

Her eyes narrowed. "I don't have time for your fun and games, Agent Dillon."

He shook his head. "I'm not an agent anymore."

"You will always be Agent Dillon, overprotective brother and the talk of the dorms to me."

"Talk of the dorms?"

She laughed. "It was embarrassing to Maura, but you were the subject of much gossip when you came to visit. Anything else?"

He shook his head.

"I should finish my edits tonight, and if you want a tour of the island, I'll be happy to do it. Tomorrow. Afternoon. No, after one."

He nodded. "I have a feeling I'll crash for a while."

She gave him one of those sultry smiles that had been driving him crazy since he'd arrived.

"Call if you need me."

If he didn't know better, he would have said she was being suggestive. While she flirted with him sometimes, he had never really taken it seriously. There was a barrier there she put up for all men. In his relationships, he needed something more. Submission from a partner did not work if the partner did not completely trust him...and he had a feeling Jillian trusted few people. Especially men.

Before he could respond, she turned and walked out the door. He couldn't help but admire the way her jeans molded to her very generous ass. Once the door shut, Dillon looked around the small living space. It was humid and hot, even with the windows open. He knew before coming that the place didn't have AC, but even living in Miami didn't prepare him for this.

He sighed as he opened the fridge and pulled out a bottle of water. Jillian had said not to worry about having any groceries at first, and she had been right. There was bread, some milk and a few eggs, along with several bottles of water. He twisted off the cap and took a long drink. Glancing at his suitcase, he realized that for once he would wait to unpack. It wasn't like him, but hell, maybe he should revel in the vacation.

Before he knew it, he'd finished off the water. He tossed it into the recycle bin Jillian had in the kitchen area. The thought of Jillian brought up her image in his mind. He wondered just how many tattoos she had and just where they led to.

He shook his head, amused with himself. It was a testament to just how tired he was that he was fantasizing about Jillian. The woman had no schedule, led a completely bohemian life-style, and was friends with his sister. She might as well be wearing a big sign that said "Off-Limits."

Conner rolled his shoulders. Damn, he was still hot. He grabbed his suitcase to find something to wear for the night but first, a cold shower. Hopefully, it would help cool him off...and take his mind off his luscious new landlady.

Jillian groaned when she heard the knocking on her door. She had been up until after two in the morning working. It was Conner Dillon's fault. He'd broken her concentration the night before. Not because he was a new tenant, but because he was Conner. Sexy Conner. But she'd gotten the edits back to her editor, and she had a week off before she had any other new work to do. Her back still hurt from the hours hunkered over her laptop. Even just rolling over hurt. She would definitely need a massage this week, or she would end up spending the next two weeks working the kinks out.

She buried her head and prayed whoever it was would leave. She was sleeping in, dammit. It couldn't be important, not really. If it was, someone would call her. More than likely it was some lost tourist. So many of them came to Hawaii thinking that all the inhabitants of the islands worked for the tourism board. While she normally didn't mind, today was just not the day she could be an ambassador of aloha.

Finally, the knocking stopped. She sighed and was almost back to sleep when the knocking started up again.

"Fuck."

She got up out of bed, barely able to see. She squinted at the clock. Dammit, it wasn't even nine am. She was going to kill someone. First, she would torture them slowly, until they begged for death. Then, she would kill them. With some effort, she stumbled to the front door.

"You're dead," she said as she opened the door. She found Conner on the other side.

Great. This was exactly what she needed. Her hair was a mess, and the man who had broken her concentration the night before was here bright and early.

"I'm sorry, but you said to come by around noon or one?"

She blinked at him. "It's not even nine."

He frowned and looked down at his watch. God, the man was gorgeous. Even in her beleaguered state, she could appreciate him. She always had. From the first time she'd met him, she had been intrigued. All that muscle and brawn packed into one delectable package was too much to resist. Throw in that he was so protective of his sister and he was downright irresistible.

Until he opened his mouth.

"It's way past noon."

She frowned at him, realizing he was being serious. Jillian grabbed his hand and pulled him closer. She looked at the watch.

"You forgot to change the time."

He blinked at her with those steel gray eyes. Damn, how could a man have such impossibly long eyelashes and look so masculine?

"What?"

"You're five hours ahead there, Dillon. Didn't you notice?"

He blinked again then looked down at her hand which still had hold of his. Heat sizzled up her arm, throughout her entire body. She released him and took a step back.

"I can't believe I didn't change my watch. Or that I didn't notice it's only nine in the morning."

She couldn't either. She'd lived with Maura in college and considered her a close friend, but she didn't know Conner that well. But what she did know was that he was always on time. He was on top of things and took control of just about every situation there was. This was just not normal for him. Now she was starting to understand why Maura was so worried.

"Sorry I woke you, I'll let you go."

She wanted that. She *needed* that, seriously. Her brain wasn't working properly. Little sleep, and now her brain had been sex sizzled by the former agent. But he was Maura's brother, and the man looked completely lost there for a second. Maura had told her that he hadn't been doing that well, but Maura tended to overreact. Still, there was no reason to be a complete bitch.

"Come on in. I'll make some coffee."

He hesitated as his gaze traveled down her body. She looked down and felt heat flare in her cheeks. Dammit, she was wearing an old T-shirt that hit her mid-thigh and nothing else.

She cleared her throat. "I'll get dressed. Come on."

He smiled, and she felt her heart do a slow roll. "You don't have to get dressed on my account."

Her cheeks got even hotter, but she ignored it. "Do you want some Kona or not?"

He nodded. She stepped back and allowed him into her home. The moment he entered her space, she knew it was a mistake. Her house was just the right size for her. But with Conner in it, it seemed small, almost miniature. He was a big man, about six foot four. She was no featherweight, but then she figured the muscled god now surveying the area for intruders also had the kind of presence that was bigger than normal.

"I'll get the coffee started. This way," she said with a nod of her head toward her kitchen. He followed her in.

"Your part of the house isn't that much bigger than mine."

She glanced at him, wondering at the tone. Shrugging, she grabbed the coffee canister and started measuring the grounds out, dumping them into the basket.

"I don't need much space. I guess if I lived with someone, it would be different."

He leaned against the counter and crossed his arms over his chest. "How so?"

"I need space to write. I need privacy. If I was living with someone here, it might be disastrous. I'm sure there would be a death."

He smiled, and again, she felt heat spike through her blood. Damn, the man was making her melt right there in her kitchen. She hoped it was just the lack of sleep. Until now, she had never even felt the urge to act on the attraction. Sure, she had fantasized. Any heterosexual woman in her right mind would. He was the stuff she wrote about in books. Confident, sexy, and she had a pretty good idea that he was a Dom. Those three things had her imagination working overtime, and for the first time, she went beyond thinking about what it would be like. This was not a good development with him being in Hawaii for a month.

She turned on the coffee pot. "I'll be right back."

He nodded, keeping his attention on her but saying nothing. Dammit, why did she like that? There was something different about him, something that was making her want to giggle like a freaking teenager. Maybe because he was looking at her differently than he ever had before.

She scooted out of the kitchen and headed to her bedroom. God, it looked like a cyclone had hit her room. She must have been really lost the last couple of days working on the book. Clothes were all over the floor and draped over the chair. She sighed, opening the dresser drawer and pulling out a pair of faded cutoffs and a T-shirt. Dammit, she thought, and she opened her lingerie drawer and grabbed a bra and a pair of panties.

Five minutes later, she was dressed, her teeth brushed, and she had her braids pulled back with a do-rag. With a deep breath, she walked out to join Conner again.

He was looking out the front window, a mug of coffee in his hand. His expression told her he was thinking of more serious things than his crazy landlady's penchant for sleeping in shirts and nothing else. He looked like the weight of the world was on his shoulders. It had always been like that as long as she could remember. He had shown up at the University of Georgia that first day with Maura, acting like a bulldog, daring anyone to say anything mean to his sister.

He had been the talk of the dorm. She hadn't been lying about that. Girls had done everything to catch his attention, but his main focus had been Maura, and in that she had admired him. She wished she'd had someone looking out for her like Maura had all those years. Strong, dependable, sexy. Okay, she wouldn't have wanted him for a brother...but a lover? Maybe. She had a feeling he had a real dominant streak and that was something she liked in a man.

For the first time in months, she felt stirrings of attraction. He wasn't her type. She liked a dominant man, but Conner was over the top. Plus, she was sure that a man like him would never be interested in a pierced and tattooed erotic romance author who ran on no schedule. Still, it didn't mean that she couldn't appreciate the beauty of the man. It was a shame that he'd chosen to wear jeans and a shirt today. She could just imagine what he looked like without a shirt. Hell, now that she thought about it, she wanted to see him like that. No shirt, a pair of board shirts, water dripping down his chiseled chest...

"Are you going to keep staring at me, or are you going to get some coffee?" he asked. He hadn't turned around, but he must have realized she had been staring at him for a while.

"I was just thinking that Maura was really lucky to have you growing up."

He turned and looked at her. "I doubt she's thinking that at the moment."

She shook her head. "You really can't blame her. You scared her."

He shrugged, and she could see why Maura said she wanted to throw things at him sometimes. He said nothing and turned around to look out the window, sipping his coffee.

"You might want to get some coffee, Jillian. You're looking a bit peaked."

She chuckled. "You don't know the half of it."

Shaking herself out of her stupor, she headed to the kitchen. She needed to quit drooling over her new tenant because nothing was going to happen with him. It would be a mistake— a total idiotic act—to sleep with him. He was a man that could fulfill her needs, and she would lose her friend in the process.

She didn't have many women friends, but Maura was a constant in Jillian's life.

She poured her coffee then took a sip, hoping the caffeine would jolt her head out of the gutter.

"So, what do you plan to do with me?"

The steamy liquid caught in her throat and she began coughing. When she finally caught her breath, she looked over at him. He was smiling at her and sipping his coffee. Now she knew he was messing with her.

Jillian picked up a napkin and wiped her mouth. "Do with you?"

"Today. You said you would show me around. You haven't changed your mind, have you?"

"No. I promised Maura I would keep my eye on you."

His smile widened. "That's interesting."

She rolled her eyes. "I thought we could drive around, maybe pick up some lunch?"

"That sounds like a plan." Then he surprised her by winking at her. "For now."

He turned and walked out of the kitchen leaving her completely aroused and thoroughly confused.

two

Conner watched Jillian as she turned onto Kamehameha Highway. It was hard not to be a little distracted by her. She had always been fascinating, but now she was in her element. Hawaii seemed to agree with her in a way the mainland never would.

He still felt a little bad about waking her up. Worse, he didn't like the fact that he hadn't realized what time it was. Hell, all he had to do was look outside. He had even been outside to go down and knock on her door and hadn't noticed the sun. He'd traveled enough to think of these things, but lately details had been escaping him.

"Have you talked to Maura today?"

He shook his head. "I have a feeling I will soon. She's being a little overprotective."

She laughed as she rolled to a stop behind a tour van. "Yeah, I have no idea where she got that from."

"What do you mean by that?"

She snorted and put the jeep in gear as the light turned green. "You were a bit...overbearing in college."

"Really?"

"Yeah. I mean, I was in my sophomore year, and Maura was my third roommate. But you knew that, right?"

He nodded, wishing he could see her eyes, but she had covered them with a pair of mirrored aviator sunglasses. Normally, they would make the woman wearing them look masculine, but on Jillian they just made her sexier.

"You were the first of my roommates' relatives to check me out."

For a second, he thought of the night before, the way she had looked with those snug jeans, barely-there T-shirt, and the way she had been dressed that morning. He was damned sure she hadn't been wearing panties under that shirt.

"What do you mean?"

"I know you did a background check on me."

"Did you tell Maura?" he asked, feeling more than a little embarrassed.

She laughed. "Do you think that Maura would have kept quiet if I had?"

He had to smile at that and the sound of her laugh. She rarely tried to hide her joy, and sometimes it was a bit contagious.

"No, I doubt that. There is one thing Maura has never been, and that's quiet."

"Tell me about it. She's a loud one. But then, I think that's why you complement each other. She lives life out loud, and you go about it very quietly. Believe me, with my family, I know how bad it can be having too much of one kind of personality."

Jillian had been right. He did snoop, so he knew about her family. Born to a white, upper-middle class mother and an

African-American superstar baseball player father, she had spent the first ten years of her life away from the crazy Bentley family of Atlanta. When her parents had died in a car crash, she'd had nowhere else to go except to that crazy Bentley family. And even though she was no longer rooming with his sister, he had kept tabs on her. He didn't know why, but for some reason he felt a need to make sure she was doing okay. Probably because she had taken care of Maura. Moving to Hawaii had been exactly what he'd expected of her. From what Conner could tell, she'd had little to no contact with her family since her grandmother had died three years ago.

"You're not mad?"

"That you snooped? Naw. I probably would have done the same for a younger sibling. And, well, Maura was...kind of naive."

"Kind of?" he asked.

"Really. I worried about her. But, she hasn't changed much."

She hadn't. Maura and he were more than ten years apart in age. It hadn't been easy taking on the task of raising her while chasing an FBI career. When she'd graduated from high school a year early, it had been a blessing and a curse. A year younger and years behind her peers in social development, she had been a lamb among wolves, but she'd had Jillian. Who, despite what some people would think about her appearance, was dependable.

"She was lucky to have you as a roommate."

She slid him a look out of the corner of her eye. He couldn't tell what she was thinking because of the glasses, but the side of her mouth kicked up.

"That was sweet of you. Just for that, I'll take you all the way down into Pearl City for some Italian food."

"Not Hawaiian?"

She shook her head. "We'll do that later. Today, and always when I finish a book, I head on down to Bravo's. It is sort of a superstition for me to follow."

"Sounds good."

"It sounds better than good; it sounds like a feast coming on. I just realized I forgot to eat lunch and dinner yesterday. It will be nice to linger around a restaurant and get the latest gossip on one of my best friends."

"There isn't much to tell."

She glanced at him. "Really? What's going on with that Zeke guy?"

"They don't like each other." He shrugged.

"Uh, you really have been working too much if you haven't noticed that they are either hooking up or preparing to."

He had worried about that but thought it was only his imagination. His best friend and his sister were opposites in every way. But knowing Jillian had picked up on it meant that it was more than just a weird feeling he had. He really didn't want to contemplate it, but he didn't have a choice. Working with the two of them made it his business. If things went badly, it could affect the company. Mainly because he would have to kill his best friend and business partner for hurting his sister.

"Oh, no. Don't get that look."

"What do you mean?"

"Your 'I am the big brother in charge' look. Maura is an adult and thankfully, no longer a virgin."

He grimaced when she said it, and she laughed. "I would rather not think about it."

"Sorry, but true. I bet you're thinking you shouldn't be here, that you should have stayed on the mainland to protect your sister from Zeke."

"No. Okay. Maybe. Part of the problem is that I work with them."

"I got a piece of information for you, Conner. I think you'd have more work protecting Zeke. You know how Maura is when she wants something, and I have a feeling she wants your best friend. Let it go, relax and enjoy Hawaii."

"I don't do vacations."

"You do now," she said with a laugh as she eased onto an elevated highway. "Now let me tell you about H-3, which is what we're on right now. Did you know that it's the most expensive highway in the US?"

"No, really?" he asked with a sarcastic edge to his tone.

"If you're going to be a jackass, I'm not telling you one of the main reasons they built it."

He glanced out the window at the tall mountains, the seemingly endless green of the rain forests. Fog clung to the tops of the mountains, so unlike what he'd expected of Hawaii. He had been here for a short time when hunting for Dee a couple of years before, but he hadn't done any sightseeing. When he thought of Hawaii, the first things that came to mind were beaches, Elvis, and Mai Tais.

This was different. Jillian had settled here, in the shadow of the mountains and some of the most beautiful scenery he had ever seen.

He glanced at her and saw that she was no longer smiling. He wanted her smiling, wanted her happy. So, he decided to give in.

"Tell me. I promise to behave."

She gave him a dazzling smile. "It was built to move troops from Kaneohe to Pearl Harbor. Before it, there wasn't a road that led straight there. Most of them went around the mountains, and all of them took the troops well out of their way."

And knowing she was on a roll, he sat back and listened to the sweet sound of her southern accent telling him about the road and the surrounding parts of the island. The cool moist air was brushing over his skin, and he felt his body relax as he drifted off to sleep.

Jillian smiled as she read over her email on her phone. Her editor had the book and would look over it one more time, and then they could send it off to be formatted.

Conner was snoring softly beside her in the passenger seat. She was sure when he woke up, he would not be too happy about it. Somewhere between the stadium and Bravo's, he'd passed out. She was sure he was tired. The trip, along with the months of hard work while opening his DC office, had worn him out. It was one of the reasons he had ended up in the ER. The other was that he was wound up so tight.

Her phone vibrated in her hand, and Maura's picture came up. Jillian slipped out of the car and answered.

"Hey, girl, what are you calling me for?" she asked.

"I wanted to check on my brother," Maura said easily. "How's he doing?"

"Considering I was up until two working on edits and he woke me up at nine, pretty good."

Maura laughed. "I'm amazed his arms are still attached."

"He didn't change the time on his watch."

There was a beat of silence.

"And he didn't realize it was the morning and not the afternoon?"

Jillian sighed. "Don't use that tone, Maura. He's fine. You know how it is when you show up here jetlagged. Add in the fact he has yet to catch up after the stint in the hospital, and he's exhausted."

"But Conner doesn't do that. He can go days without sleep." Her voice was filled with concern. She knew Maura well enough to know that she would worry herself sick for no reason.

"Maura, let it go. Remember, Conner's edging his way up to forty. He's getting older, and running around on adrenaline takes a toll on an older body. When guys get older, you have to let them have some down time."

"So nice to hear you care, Jillian," he said from behind her.

She closed her eyes and realized that she had been so concerned about soothing her friend's worries that she hadn't heard him get out of the car.

"Was that Conner?" Maura asked.

"Yes." She opened her eyes and turned around. He was leaning against the back of her jeep, watching her. She couldn't tell if he was mad or not.

"I take it that's Maura?" he asked.

She nodded.

"Let me talk to her."

Without thinking, she gave over the phone. And as soon as she did, she was annoyed. He didn't ask, he commanded, and that irritated the living hell out of her. But since he already had it and was soothing Maura's worries now, Jillian figured the point was moot.

"I told you, I'll be fine."

He was quiet as he listened. "Zeke's friend is there already?" He frowned. "That was fast."

He grew quiet again, but since he was concentrating on the conversation, she was free to study him. She'd done so a lot when she was in college. For a man who had a busy FBI career, he had always found the time to visit his sister. And he had always included her when they went out. It was hard for a twenty-something not to be impressed. He was quiet, dominating, and gorgeous. Now, though, she was older. She should be able to appreciate how attractive he was without drooling, but her brain was already refusing to work.

"According to Jillian, this is the best Italian on the island." Quiet again. "Yes, Bravo's." He glanced at her and smiled. "She didn't kill me even though I woke her up, and she's feeding me, so I think I'm okay."

She could hear Maura's voice babbling along and Conner showing once again how patient he was with his sister.

"No. Leave us alone. You wanted me to come here, so let it go, Maura. Love you. Behave."

He hung up even though Jillian was pretty sure Maura was still talking. He held the phone out to her, and she took it.

"You had to tell her I lost track of the time?"

She grimaced as she grabbed her purse out of the back seat. "Sorry about that. That's what you get when you wake me up in the morning. I'm not good on only a few hours of sleep."

He rocked back on his heels as he watched her lock the door. "She's convinced I need to see a doctor while I'm here."

"What did your doctor say?" she asked.

"Only if I get light-headed or feel any more chest pains."

"Then tell your sister to get bent."

He snorted. "Like that would work."

She sighed. "You were always too easy when it came to Maura."

"What does that mean?"

"She could get you to do anything, admit it. She still can."

He shrugged.

"Your sister is the greatest. I love her like she is my own flesh and blood. Actually, better than my own flesh and blood, considering the Bentleys. But she was always bigger than life. If you don't take her down a peg, she'll roll right over you. She might be part of the reason you had the pains to begin with."

She slipped her purse strap over her head to rest it on her shoulder and started walking to Bravo's.

"Did you tell her that?" he asked, accusation easy to hear in his voice.

"No. I didn't. But someone needs to. I'm not saying that a lot of this isn't your fault. Hell, you're a workaholic. Add in the fact you've decided to expand the business, then you have issues."

"You have a lot of opinions for someone who hasn't seen me for years."

She saw the manager open the front door. "Come on. I need some food if we're going to argue."

She started walking toward the door again.

"We're not arguing."

She threw her hands up in the air but did not stop walking. She could already smell the garlic, and her mouth was watering.

"Oh my God, you are insane. Come on, the garlic bread is calling my name."

Conner glanced around the restaurant and silently admitted Jillian was right. The strange little spot did have some good food. Two restaurants sat one on top of the other. The one upstairs seemed to be a diner of some sort. Within moments of them being seated, the place was packed. The bread was probably the most delicious thing he'd had in months.

"So, you opened an office in DC. I thought you hated DC."

He studied her. "Are you trying to irritate me?"

She laughed. "No, but I figured that's all you've been living and breathing for a few months. You probably have nothing else to talk about."

He hated to admit it, but it was the truth. He hadn't had a social life, let alone a date, in months. He'd been so busy running back and forth between DC and Miami, he couldn't take the time to deal with it.

"I know a lot of people there. So, it's easier to hire. With the way the government is going with contracts, it will be easy to pick up some more work."

"Are you going to leave someone in charge, or are you going to run yourself into the ground again?"

He smiled. "You have no filter, do you?"

She laughed, this time a little louder, and it gained some attention from the group of military men sitting a few booths down. They had been throwing looks their way since the four men had been seated. He hated to admit it but he didn't like that. He frowned at them, and they ignored him.

"I don't. I used to, but then I said fuck it. Life's too short not to let people know what you think."

"Ah, well, yes, actually, I hired an old buddy of mine from the FBI to head it up. He just retired and has a lot of experience in surveillance."

She nodded. "And so you'll stay in Miami? I hate that town."

"Why?"

"Too many people."

He chuckled. "You live on Oahu. There are over three quarters of a million people on the island."

"You saw where I live, right? Not a lot of people around there."

She was right about that. It was sort of in its own little corner, without many people around. There were locals, but not many tourists that he had seen.

"What are your plans here? Seeing that you've never been here before."

"I've been here before."

That caught her off guard. It took her a couple of seconds to recover and the waitress returned with their meals. She set down a generous helping of ravioli in front of him. The salad Jillian got was enough for a small nation to eat.

When they were alone, she said, "I thought this was your first time?"

She sounded disappointed by it for some odd reason.

"No, I had to come for a job a couple of years ago."

Her eyes lit with comprehension. "Oh, that old case of yours. Okay. That was right before I moved here. Well, what did you see last time?"

He thought about the trip to Rough 'n Ready, then the race

to follow Dee and Micah back to the mainland. "Nothing really."

She stopped eating. "What do you mean?"

"I was here for work. I didn't have time."

She set down her fork. "This is Hawaii. You make time."

He shook his head. He knew it was easy to say something like that when you were only responsible for yourself. But he had people depending on him.

"I had to leave right away when Dee's brother stole her away."

She shook her head. "Well, then I can take you around. It's fun to show someone the island. I did it with your sister a few months ago."

"You act like you don't have a lot of visitors."

She shrugged and dug into her salad again. "Not really. I don't invite my family because, well, because they don't know where I live. Friends in the industry, a lot of them are married and can't run to Hawaii at the drop of a hat. And again, a lot of them have no idea where I live."

He knew there was more to it than that. Something bigger was there. Maura had told him that although her family lived in Atlanta, Jillian had not gone home that often when they were at college. No one really visited, and he uncovered a lot of contempt from everyone in the family when he had her checked out.

"So, you think to use me as a guinea pig?"

"It'll be fun. I just turned in a book, so I have some time on my hands. I can show you all kinds of things."

He wouldn't doubt that. Maybe he hadn't had enough sleep, or maybe he had been too long without a woman, but he couldn't fight the heat that seemed to flare now every time she was near. When she was in college, she had been attractive. Now over the age of thirty, she was stunning.

"Okay."

"Do you want to do the touristy things, or do you want to see things like a local?"

"Local. I don't need glittery tourist areas. I do better in normal surroundings."

She laughed again, and there went the dance in his blood. Damn, the woman was a bit intoxicating, and he was feeling light-headed. He knew it wasn't from the issues he was having before, but from the woman he was spending time with.

"Tell you what. We'll hit the important tourist spots, but then I'll show you places the *kama'aina* like to go."

"The what?"

"The *kama'aina*, the locals. We're *haoles*, newbies to the island."

"You've lived here for almost two years."

"For the Hawaiians, that isn't long enough. So, being that it's past time for the swap meet, we can go up to Sunset Beach. The surf report was good today."

"I didn't bring my trunks."

"Of course you didn't, we were just going to lunch."

He shook his head. "No, with me. I didn't bring any with me to Hawaii."

"You came to Hawaii without any swim trunks?"

He felt a wave of embarrassment wash over him.

"I just didn't think of it."

"Well, first things first. We'll hop on over to Pearlridge and grab you a pair, then we'll head on up. Then, we can have some fun on the beach."

Jillian in a bathing suit was going to be a hard thing to

ignore, but he couldn't turn her down. She looked so happy, and dammit, it had been a long time since he'd taken a day just to play in the sand. So, he agreed.

"Sounds good."

She gave him another brilliant smile, and he felt as if he owned the world. Now all he had to do was keep his hands off her while they were there.

three

Jillian sighed as she leaned back on the sand and enjoyed the heat of the sun on her skin. The salty scent of the Pacific tickled her nose as did the sweet aroma of the coconut oil the sunbathers wore. From the moment they had stepped on the beach, she had felt her body start to relax.

"You look like you're in your element," Conner said. She glanced at him and then closed her eyes. If she looked at him too much without a shirt on, she might do something crazy. All that hard muscle, lean and sculpted...It made her want to run her tongue all over him.

"I do like the beach. I love that I can walk down the street from my house and out onto a beach."

"You could do that in Miami."

She glanced at him. "Yeah, I could. But then, it isn't this pretty."

He studied the landscape. "I guess that's true. I don't know if there is a beach on the mainland that is this pretty."

"California has some nice beaches, but I just love it here.

The Hawaiians make it just that much better. They appreciate what they have."

He looked like he didn't believe her, but he said nothing. He had been like that for as long as she had known him. Now, though, it was bothering her. Since she'd put on the white bikini, she hadn't been able to shake the feeling that he was looking at her weirdly. It was as if he was trying to figure something out about her.

"The waves aren't that big today."

She shook herself out of the stupor. "They'll grow later today. And you have to admit, they're bigger than what you have in Miami."

For a second, he didn't say anything. Then he asked, "What?"

"The waves, they're bigger than in Miami."

He relaxed. "Oh. Yeah. I was never a big surfer, though."

She nodded and lay back again. "I usually try and come out here with someone because I tend to fall asleep in the sun."

"Mick or Adam?"

She nodded. "I'm such a sound sleeper when I'm warm enough. Someone could probably come up to me and steal everything I have here, including my bathing suit, and I wouldn't notice."

"I think I'll hit the water," he said abruptly. Without waiting for a response, he jumped up and walked out to the water. She rose to rest her weight on her elbows and watched him. The man was put together like a freaking god. Hell, she found his legs attractive. And, just like most good-looking men, he was getting better looking with age. There were a few little wisps of gray in his hair, but for the most part, he looked like he was just in his early thirties, not approaching forty.

Totally wrong for her. *So wrong*. But she couldn't help thinking that there was a hint of attraction in the way he looked at her. She was pretty sure he liked the way she looked in a bikini, but he wasn't like other guys. He considered her off-limits for a few reasons. Number one was his sister. And then there was the issue that he liked to have every day planned out. Jillian did that with writing, but in her personal time, she liked to go with the flow.

She brushed the thoughts of Conner and his feelings about her away. Thinking about him was just going to cause her troubles, and she had enough of those to keep her busy.

Conner welcomed the cold water as he jumped into it. He dove under, praying it would help him get himself under control. He came up for air and deliberately did not look toward the beach. If he did, he wouldn't be able to do anything but stare at her.

Jillian was an attractive woman. There was a spark within her that he was sure no heterosexual man could ignore. But for some strange reason, he felt drawn to her like never before. Was it because of his recent problems? It could be. Conner knew he had been called a control freak. Hell, he *was* a control freak. It was one of the reasons he was good at his job, and why he ended up in the hospital.

With Jillian, he didn't seem to have much control. It had been less than a day and he was already becoming obsessed. When she had donned that little white excuse for a bathing suit, his first instinct had been to cover her up. Every bit of the moisture had dried up in his mouth. All that cocoa skin exposed made his fingers itch to touch. She wasn't a skinny woman, thank God. She had hips and an ass—lord did she have an ass. Her breasts were full and firm. And, dammit, the tattoos were killing him. Along with the belly-button piercing. He had never gone for a woman with piercings and tats, but with Jillian, he wanted to trace his tongue over her ink then work his way down her stomach.

Off-limits.

He had to keep repeating the phrase over and over in his head. At some point, it might sink in. Getting involved with her would cause more problems than he could even fathom. She was one of his sister's best friends. Maura didn't have a lot of girlfriends, and he had an idea that Jillian was the same way. Also, what if things went wrong before he left? That would be an issue. Dealing with a breakup could really ruin his relationship with Jillian.

He needed to keep his hands off her. That was all there was to it.

He looked back up at her lying on the sand and watched two big guys approaching her. She smiled up at the men, and all the ideas he had about steering clear of her evaporated when one of the men reached down and yanked her up into his arms. She screamed then laughed as the behemoth headed to the water with her. A flash of anger, mixed with the sharp taste of jealousy, whipped through him and had Conner marching to the shore.

"I think you need to put the woman down," he said as he approached them.

The two guys blinked at him. Jillian smiled. "No worries, Conner. These are my friends, Mick and Adam. This is my new tenant, Conner Dillon."

The idiot holding her said, "Oh, Maura's brother. Your sister is a sweetheart."

He narrowed his eyes at the Neanderthal. He didn't know if he was more irritated with the fact that he smiled when he said Maura's name or that he thought he could manhandle Jillian. That it might be the latter bothered him more.

"I said you might want to put the lady down."

The brute shared a look with his friend, who was trying not to smile. Then he turned back and faced Conner. "No harm done, I just know how Jillian is about water."

"What do you mean how I am about water? Is this some kind of racist thing?" she asked.

He could hear her laughter, but Conner ignored her. He just didn't like the fact that the asshole hadn't put her down. With another look at his friend, he set her down on the ground.

"See ya later, Jill," Mick said and walked away. His friend Adam, though, kept smiling at him, and then gave Jillian a kiss on the cheek and followed after Mick.

She crossed her arms under her breasts. "That was stupid. Mick was only fooling around."

He said nothing because he was starting to realize how stupid he looked now. Her friend had been fooling around, and he could tell from the easy friendship between them that they knew each other well. The problem that gave him was that he had a feeling they might have slept together.

"I didn't know that."

He was pretty sure she rolled her eyes, but she had her sunglasses on again. "And, what did you think he was doing?"

Okay, now that he had to explain himself, it sounded idiotic.

She huffed out a breath and turned around to walk back up

the beach. Thanks to her irritation and the sand, her hips swung even more than usual. Her tiny bikini bottom wasn't much of a cover for her generously curved ass. All the anger he had felt now dissolved into lust. Jesus, the woman should come with a warning sign. Men's heads turned as she walked past them, but she paid them no attention.

"I can understand Maura's comments now. Please tell me you aren't like this with her? Do you see me as your little sister you have to protect?"

"Good God, no." The idea she thought that left him slightly ill. No way in hell did he see her as a little sister.

She glanced at him before bending over to grab her towel and her beach mat. His eyes almost crossed.

"We don't have to leave."

"Actually, I think we should. You really haven't had enough sleep, and I need to work on a few emails to my PA."

He wanted to argue with her, keep her there as long as possible, but he didn't want to look like an idiot.

"Okay, but next time we go out, it's my treat."

She gave him that blinding smile that he felt all the way to his soles. The woman was definitely lethal.

"Anytime, bruddah."

Jillian grabbed her backpack and sunglasses and headed to the door. She was ready to make sure Conner got out today. They hadn't spent much time together the last few days, mainly because she had resurfaced to a ton of emails she'd ignored while working on her edits. There was cover art for her next three books to deal with and the promotional plan for her next release. Being self-published was work. But it was work she was happy to have.

She danced up the stairs and knocked on Conner's door.

He opened it, and she gave him a smile. "Let's go, Conner."

He said nothing as he stepped out and looked around.

"Isn't it kind of early for you?"

"Don't be an ass. I had a twitter chat this morning, and it was on mainland time. So, I was up. Plus, I want to take you to the swap meet."

He frowned, and she could almost hear the wheels turning in his head, trying to come up with a reason not to go.

"I'm not sure that's my kind of place."

"You wanted to hang out with locals. Let's go. It's the place to get everything you could ever imagine in Hawaii."

"Really?"

"If you don't come with me, I will call Maura and tell her I'm worried about you."

He gave her one of his long-considering looks. "That's mean of you."

"I never said I was nice. It's a mistake that many men have made before you. Meet you down at the jeep in five."

She didn't wait for an answer. Once she got to the jeep, she unlocked it and slipped in, waiting for him. It had been tough to ignore him up there the last few days, but she had. He had gone out a couple of times, asked for directions, but she hadn't been invited. Nor had she invited herself. They had some strangeness between them after the scene on the beach, and she guessed they both had needed space.

When she had talked to Adam about it, he had asked if they were sleeping together. And, she thought back, he had said they would. Soon. Until she'd talked to Adam, she had thought the attraction was one-sided. Apparently she had been wrong.

The door opened, and Conner got in, still frowning.

"Get over it."

He gave her a surprised glance. "No, my sister called. Seems like that Rory character is causing some issues."

"Oh, Rory. He's Zeke's friend, right?"

"Not sure. Just, the way she talks about him...like there is something bothering her."

"Yeah, two hot Irish guys—that would bother me, too."

She pulled out on Kam Highway and wondered if he really did see Maura as a little girl still. She glanced in his direction and noticed the confused expression.

"You do know she is a grown-up, right?"

"Shut up. You don't have an older brother. Thinking about my sister wanting a guy—"

"Or guys."

When he said nothing, she glanced at him again. He'd closed his eyes. "Ugh. I don't even want to think about that. My sister is still fifteen years old in my heart."

Oh no. What woman could resist a guy who said things like that?

"She's lucky to have you."

She knew her voice sounded thick. She could feel him study her, but she didn't want to look at him. Through years of living with the most fucked-up family in Georgia, she'd learned to hide emotion. She didn't like anyone to see her weakness.

"So, you think I need to go to this swamp meet?"

She snorted. "Swap meet, and yes. You need to get your sister something there. And, there's Lin's Market, Tom Lin, and Hawaiian Ice. You cannot beat that, bruddah."

"Sounds like a plan."

She hit the gas to speed around a minivan full of kids. "And you like those?"

"I'm better with rules than without."

"And that's why you're a Dom."

Again, she felt his study. "How did you know?"

"I write erotic romance, Con. Seriously, did you think I wouldn't pick up on it?"

He shifted in his seat. "I'm not used to people knowing about that part of my life."

"You are a practicing Dom, right?"

"First, I don't have to *practice* at anything." His sardonic tone made her laugh.

"Okay. But, you are a Dom. I didn't read that wrong."

"No. I just haven't had the time to get to a club lately."

"Work has interfered with more than just the typical social part of your life, huh?"

He didn't say anything for a moment. Jillian glanced at him and noticed he was studying the fog hanging around the mountains. He was flexing his jaw as if he was grinding his teeth. Did she push him too far? She had a habit of that with men. More than once she had stepped over the line of what she should ask them. Or what they thought she should ask them. It was a problem she had lived with all her life. Her grandmother had always said she asked too many questions. Problem was that her parents had encouraged it. Her father had constantly marveled at her curiosity and said that it showed she was brilliant.

"That has been a problem."

For a second, she didn't know he was talking to her.

"I can see that it would be. Something like that takes trust, and you have to build the relationship."

She sensed he shook his head as they went through the darkness of the first tunnel through the mountains.

"Not really. If you're a regular member of a club, you can easily find a sub for the night. There are people who have no problem hooking up for play for a while."

"That's not you though, Conner."

As soon as she said it, she knew it to be the truth. He wasn't a man who would want a sub for the night. He would want a woman completely and absolutely involved, one who submitted only to him.

Heat threaded through her veins as they hit sunlight again. Damn, the man was too tempting to resist. Almost.

"Yeah, not my thing. When I was younger, yes. At my advanced age, though, I find it tiring hitting the clubs."

"You are *not* old."

He chuckled. "My sister and my doctor disagree with you. But, I would say that I'm not old, and definitely not settled. Just —the club scene is not what I want. I'm sure a lot of people my age think the same way."

"And some of them don't. Some of them will always hit the clubs."

"Yeah, I guess. But then, different strokes and all that."

"I would have never known you to be so laid-back."

"Shit," he said when the full sun hit them. He pulled down his sunglasses. "Sort of hits you without warning."

She laughed. "Yeah it does."

"Back to that, I am laid-back as long as someone isn't breaking the law and isn't involved in my life. I don't think I want to know what goes on in most bedrooms. Live and let live."

"Wow, that's...different than I expected."

She sensed his amusement and looked over at him. He was smiling at her. The sun was picking up the silvery threads that wove through his hair. Why did she find that attractive?

"Yeah, but then you don't know me that well. You know me through Maura, and I feel differently—or did—about what she should be doing. I had to raise her and make sure she didn't do something stupid."

"Have you ever known her to do something stupid?"

Then, as soon as she asked the question, they both started laughing. "Okay, yeah, she is kind of goofy."

"And she was naïve, especially when she got to Georgia."

"She was, but she was focused. At the time, she liked guys, but she just didn't have time for them. Didn't want to make the time for them."

"Well, she had you. And you looked out for her."

She pulled into the Aloha Stadium and into the shortest line to pay for parking. "Not any more than any other person would have."

After giving the woman her two bucks, she drove around to the other side of the stadium and parked. When she turned off the car, she realized he was staring at her.

"What?"

"Not everyone would have done what you did. A lot of people would have let her make some really stupid mistakes, but you didn't."

She brushed that away. "Naw, she would have been fine."

He shook his head, not breaking eye contact with her. "No. She might have, but she also would have made some really stupid mistakes. You saved her from that. It was much easier to do my job knowing she was living with you."

Something warm unfurled in her chest then spread to the

rest of her body. She swallowed the lump that had formed in her throat. Feeling giddy because of a simple compliment was just silly, but she couldn't help it. She valued Conner's opinion on things, mainly because she respected him. Not many men would have done what he did with his sister, but a good man did. Conner was definitely a good man.

Before she could think better of it, she leaned across and gave him a kiss on the cheek.

"Thanks."

He looked a bit stunned by the gesture, and she started to feel like an idiot. He just kept staring at her. She pushed the feelings aside and decided that they both needed space.

"Come on. Let's go spend some of your money."

He hesitated, then nodded and got out of the car. She drew in a deep breath, released it, and then grabbed her purse.

She would be better with the activity around them and a cup of Kona. Maybe, just maybe, she could forget the weirdness of the situation and move on.

Brushing away her worries, she smiled at him. "Let's go."

four

Conner watched Jillian haggle over the price of a beach towel with a vendor with a new appreciation. It was a skill he would have never guessed she had. He knew with her money she really didn't have to worry about the price. She lived comfortably, but apparently she liked to argue. As he watched her settle her hands on her hips, he realized she liked to argue a lot.

He normally didn't like women who argued. Women with a backbone—that was another matter. In fact, he didn't like the "wilting willow" type. He liked women who were strong and independent. Arguing for the sake of arguing wasn't his thing. With Jillian, he didn't seem to mind. In fact, the few times they'd argued over things, he'd found it stimulating. The idea of an argument actually had his arousal humming.

When she finished, she walked over to him with a bright smile on her face. "I love winning."

"You saved a dollar," he pointed out.

She shrugged. "I still won."

He laughed and followed her along as she made her way through the collection of tents that made up the swap meet. It had looked more like a scene from *M*A*S*H* when they had first driven up. Tents wrapped around the parking lot of the stadium several rows deep. But when they had walked into the middle of them, the place had come alive. Jillian had been right. A person could find just about anything they wanted in these tents. Purses, towels, kitchen items, suitcases, toys—and holy lord—shirts. There were more shirts than a person should see in a lifetime. It was a tourist's wet dream come to life.

"So, you bring all your tenants here to shop?"

She worked her way around a couple pushing a buggy.

"No, but then I have locals a lot of times. Or military guys. I do tend to get them up there because I am so close to Kaneohe, but also a little ways away. I guess a break from work every now and then is good. And I will do weeks, so I get military families coming or going."

"You have a lot of contact with the military?"

"Hard not to on the island, but yeah, I like to rent to them. Rarely is anything damaged and they pay on time. If anything goes wrong, I can always go to the military and get compensated to a point."

Sensible. Another contradiction. Just when he thought he might have her figured out, she changed and went off in another direction. She stopped at a tent with table after table of food.

"This is Lin's. I have to come here at least once a month to get some pineapple crack."

She beelined her way to an area in front of the cash register. From what he could tell, all the locals knew her, and this tent was no different. She picked through the bags and found one she liked. He looked over the food and found the strangest combination of Asian food he had ever found in one place. He had done time overseas, so he knew how to eat like a local, but it was just odd to find it all in one tent.

She went up to the counter with a big bag of what looked like salt, and a bag of what looked like diced pineapple.

"Morning, Jillian, how are you doing?"

"Pretty good. Showing a *haole* the way around the swap meet. It's his first time."

"And of course you bring him here," the older man said with a smile as he glanced at Conner. "Aloha."

"Aloha," he said, still feeling weird using a word that seemed foreign to him. He had seen movies where they had used it, but it was odd to use it in his everyday conversation.

"A trip to the swap meet isn't complete without a stop by Lin's. At least, not for me."

"That's because you are *akamai*."

"That I am," Jillian said with a smile. She paid for the items and then they walked out of the tent. "*A hui hou*."

"What did he call you?" Conner asked.

She flashed him a smile. "Smart. And then the *a hui hou* is sort of like 'see you later.'"

He nodded as she handed him the bag that had the salt in it. "The salt is for your sister. Although, she could easily order it online."

"You really are like a local."

Jillian shook her head. "Don't let them hear you say that. I'm still a *haole* like you."

"You've lived here for years."

She shrugged. "I came here a few years ago because Maura wouldn't shut up about it. Family was starting to get on my nerves, and I just didn't have the patience to deal with them anymore. So, I took a break. Then I fell in love. It was the first place in years where I have fit in, where when I said home, it felt right."

He knew what she was talking about. Or he thought he did. Many would look at her life and say she was lucky. The daughter of parents who loved her, and when the worst thing that could have happened did, she found herself living with rich family members. But he knew better. He knew that she had been taken on as the child that no one wanted, and while they had raised her, he knew from her comments that she hadn't had a great teenage experience. They were not only strange, but they were not welcoming. Apparently, she found her place to live.

They stopped at a food stand and she ordered them both some coffee. While she was paying for their drinks, it hit him that he didn't consider Miami home. Not really home. Sure, Maura made it more so, but there was that connection he had been missing since he left home for college. Almost forty and he still hadn't found it.

"How about a tattoo?" she asked, pulling him out of his thoughts.

He choked on the drink of coffee he'd just taken. The warm liquid shot up his nose, and he winced. She handed him a napkin.

"What?" he asked.

She smiled and nodded to a tent on the other side of him.

"It's just henna. Don't look scared."

"I'm not scared. I'm just not into tattoos on me."

She pulled her glasses down on her nose so she could look over the top of them. "What about on other people?"

He could tell from the sparkle in her eyes that she was fucking with him. He looked down her arms at a sleeve of tattoos that must have taken hours to get. "Depends on the person. I especially like yours."

"Really?"

"Yeah. That and your belly-button ring."

Her lips curved as she pushed the glasses back up and turned to walk away. The woman moved like a freaking temptress. He knew it was innate to her, like breathing. She didn't do it on purpose. That didn't mean he could ignore it. His hands itched to touch, to tease, to spank. That full ass swinging in her barely-there shorts...he was sure the lack of blood in his brain wasn't good for his health.

He caught up to her. "So, is your belly the only place you're pierced?"

"Wouldn't you like to know?"

He slipped his hand around her upper arm and gently tugged her to the side of a tent at the end of one of the rows, out of the pedestrian traffic. It was heating up, the air stifled by the arrangements of the vendors, and the humidity was rising by the minute. The scent of her filled his senses.

"Yeah, I kind of do want to know where else you're pierced."

She smiled up at him, and he could tell she was going to brush him off. The Dom in him was already beating his way out. He had lain dormant for months, but with Jillian around, those dominant tendencies were surfacing again.

She patted his cheek. "I only share that with intimate friends."

Jillian turned to leave, but he grabbed her arm again.

"Don't mess with me, Jillian. I don't like it, not that way."

Her eyes narrowed as she looked down at his hand on her upper arm.

"If you're not interested, just say 'leave me the fuck alone, Conner.'"

He waited, holding his breath. He hadn't meant to challenge her, hadn't known this was so important right now. It was. More than he had ever expected, it was beyond that now. Why this woman, right now, he had no idea. But the need he had building in him was starting to take over any sane thought he had. He knew right now if he didn't have her soon, there was a good chance he might just go a little insane. If she said to fuck off, he would be screwed.

When she didn't say anything, Conner let loose the breath and nodded. "Good, then we understand each other. Just know that when I ask you that question again, I will expect an answer."

With that he released her, waited for her to walk, and then followed her into the path of the shoppers again.

She didn't say anything for a few minutes as they strolled through another set of tents. Then she said, "That wasn't an invitation."

"What?" he asked, knowing just what she meant.

"Just because I didn't say it, it wasn't an invitation."

"Understood. Just as long as you know that from now on out, I believe I have every right to work on getting that invitation."

She stopped and looked up at him. She hid her eyes behind those sunglasses, and it was still bothering him. With Jillian, he always felt he was missing something she was hiding. Not on purpose, not really. But he had a feeling she had spent a lot of her time hiding a lot of things from most people.

"Pretty cocky, aren't you?" she asked with humor threading her voice.

48

He smiled. "What can I say? You bring it out in me."

She groaned. "Oh, that was bad."

"You gave me the setup, so you can blame yourself."

"I might have, but it doesn't mean you needed to go there." She opened the bag of pineapple bites. "Here, take one."

He did and instantly knew why she called them pineapple crack. Sweet, tart, and as soon as he finished that one, he needed another. He grabbed a few more as they started to walk again.

"That should be illegal," he said. "I think if I had those every day, I might gain fifty pounds in a week."

She laughed, and the sound of it had his heart doing more than a little two-step. She never giggled or muffled her happiness. It was always out there for you to hear...and see. "Yeah, I told you, crack. What are you going to buy Maura?"

"Buy?"

"You have to take her something. You always did."

Then he remembered making sure that he had something for her each time he visited her at college. He heard the wistfulness in Jillian's voice but he wasn't going to push anymore today. He didn't want to scare her completely off.

"I haven't thought of it. I rarely go out on a job, so I am sort of out of practice."

She nodded. "We better get her something so you don't forget. She'll whine if you come home with nothing."

He chuckled as he slipped his hands into the pockets of his shorts. "You do know my sister well."

"Yep, but then I'm good at reading a person's character. My dad said I got it from him."

She rarely talked about her parents, so any bit of information she gave him, he was going to latch on to. "Your father?"

"Dad said he had to be careful when he got to the game.

People were trying to use him left and right. New people he met, old friends. But, he said the moment he met my mother, he knew she was interested in him for him."

"Really, how?"

She gave him a blinding smile. "My mother had no idea who he was."

"Your mother didn't know who he was?"

"Yeah. Until she met Dad, Mom paid little to no attention to sports. Dad was a little put out that he had to try and woo her without what he considered his biggest selling point."

He chuckled. "I can imagine."

"It took him a while, but he got her attention. Then they were married less than a year later, I came two years after that."

She eased him over to a tent that had a lot of little knick-knacks that Maura would love. It struck him then that this was the one thing he wanted to do. He wanted to be with Jillian, looking through the offerings and just having a lazy day shopping. She was smiling at him, teasing him, and he knew this is where he needed to be.

"I think she would like this one," she said, holding up a hand-carved turtle, but he barely noticed it. Instead, he was looking at her smiling at him, and he felt something shift inside his chest.

"Conner?"

He shook his head and focused on the turtle. "Yeah, I think she would love it."

The moment over now, he followed her into the tent as he watched her dive into another haggling session.

"You think he's okay, right?" Maura asked for the third time during the five minutes they'd been on the phone.

Jillian started to rub her temple again and tried not to scream. No wonder Conner was stressed. Just the short time she had been on the phone with her old friend had Jillian's blood pressure starting to rise. The concern was not normal for Maura. She had always worried about Conner, but not like this. Jillian had a feeling that this was not just because of what happened. This had been building for a while, in Jillian's opinion.

Yes, Conner worked in a high-stress job. He didn't really take time off. That was a worry for a man who was so tightly wound. Now, though, Jillian was wondering just how much of the issue was caused by Maura. Right now, she was ready to strangle her best friend.

"He's fine. He's been here for a few days, no problems. In fact, I took him to the swap meet a couple of days ago. He had a great time."

There was a pause.

"A great time shopping?"

"Yes. I needed to pick up some stuff, including salt for you. It was kind of fun to get out of the house."

"You went with my brother, right?" Maura asked.

Jillian laughed. "Yes. I really didn't give him a choice."

He had been stiff and formal at first, but soon she'd gotten him interested in haggling prices and chatting with the locals. And he had made her go gooey inside. When he had shown the dominant side of his personality, she'd almost dissolved into a puddle of lust. On top of that, she was beginning to realize that Conner was a man she wouldn't just enjoy in bed. He was a man she could enjoy hanging out with. That wasn't that common of a thing.

"You need something to do to get your mind off your brother. He is looking good, and he is having a good time. He bought you a present."

"Wait, what did he buy me?"

"It's a surprise." And it had been sweet watching him trying to decide what to buy Maura. It was hard not to admire a brother who loved his sister so much. "Go find a guy to play with. What about Zeke?"

She sighed. "Rory's in town."

"And?"

"They're lovers."

That brought her up short. "Oh, I thought Zeke was heterosexual. I mean, you've slept with him."

"Once, and it was good, but he doesn't like BDSM. Sometimes he likes men. It's an odd relationship."

"So, he's bi." She shrugged. "That shouldn't bother you."

"No, but it's like he wants to keep Rory and me separate. It isn't like they try to hide that they're sleeping together, but he won't leave us alone."

Odd. "What's Rory like?"

Maura made a humming noise.

Jillian smiled. "That good?"

"Yeah. Worse, I know he's a Dom. It makes me want to take a big bite out of his ass every time I see him."

"And I take it that Zeke disagrees?"

"Yeah. He's so uptight. You should have seen his reaction when I said something about a threesome. He was so pissed."

Jillian had a feeling it was another kind of emotion. She had gotten to meet Zeke a few times, and she was pretty sure that he was in love with Maura. Now, with this old boyfriend who is a Dom...he wouldn't have brought him along if Zeke hadn't wanted to at least try a ménage. But telling Maura would be a waste of time.

"I don't know what to do, and he makes me feel guilty for wanting him. But, dammit, they both have those Irish accents, and it just kills me."

"I think you just need to let it happen. Don't force it."

"But you know I like a plan."

Jillian rolled her eyes. Maura did like a good plan, and she tried to plan everything out. From the time she got up in the morning until the time she went to bed, Maura had her life planned. That was one thing brother and sister had in common.

"Well, go forth and get some booty. I am taking care of your brother. He is actually getting some relaxing time in, and he has a bit of a tan. Which is odd because the man lives in Miami, and he looked like an albino when he arrived."

She laughed. "What are you doing tonight?"

"Conner's going out tonight. He apparently knows someone here from his FBI days. He left about an hour ago to meet up with him. I'm heading into Honolulu to go to Rough 'n Ready. By the way, thanks for hooking me up with Micah Ross. He's going to let me come in and observe for research."

"You might find someone you like there."

"I'm sure I will. But I told you, not my kind of thing." Not really. Jillian knew that she wanted—almost needed—a Dom in her bedroom. She knew enough about the subject, but she also knew her one big hang up. Trust.

"Call me and let me know how things are going, and I want to know what happens at the club."

She had to promise three or four times before Maura would

actually hang up. With a sigh, she tugged her shirt and pants off. She'd already slapped on a little makeup, so all she needed was clothes that fit her. As she looked through her closet, her family cell phone rang. She thought about ignoring it, but it was kind of late for an East Coast call.

She saw the number and sighed. "Hello, Blanche."

"Have you talked to Charles?"

No hello, how are you doing? Just give me my fucking money. Or rather, give me my son's fucking money.

"I did, and he said Brent would just have to deal with it on his own."

"How is he supposed to live?"

"Live?"

"He isn't like you."

She sat on her bed as her head started to throb. If Hindus were right about reincarnation, she must have been a total bitch in her last lifetime.

"Really?"

Jillian knew what was coming next. Most of the family could care less that she was half black, but with Blanche, it was very important.

"You come from the working class. You know how to work."

"Newsflash, Blanche, so did Mom. In fact, isn't that how she met my father?"

There were a few moments of silence on the phone. Jillian didn't normally let them know they got to her. But she was so damned tired of them putting her down because her father made a better life for himself. Most people thought her father was a great man.

"How is he going to survive?"

Blanche was so dramatic. The whole family was. It was like living with the fucking Barrymores.

"Maybe sell one of those motorcycles of his? That should be able to get him a few bucks. I have something to do tonight. I have to go."

Without waiting for an answer, she hung up and threw the phone on her bed. Dammit, Blanche had ruined the good vibe she'd had from her time with Conner. A little shopping, and a little flirting with a very gorgeous man. Dammit, she hated her family. She wanted to just walk away. Not for the first time, she damned her grandmother. Legally, she could do it. It would be messy, but it would make her life easier.

She fell back on her mattress. She wouldn't, though, and that bitch of a grandmother knew it. There was one thing her parents had instilled in her and that was duty. Shit.

Jillian sat up and shook off the irritation. She left her family cell sitting on the bed as she went to get ready. She wasn't going to let them ruin her good day.

Conner looked around the club. Even for a Tuesday night, it was buzzing. Lots of customers, and with a special "bring your cake and eat it, too" party going on, lots of cake. In fact, he could smell the sugar standing fifty feet away.

"Whatcha think?"

He looked at Dee Ross and tried to see her as the woman she had become. Their association had been brief when he had been ordered to protect her all those years ago. It was hard to believe she was grown-up and married. A lot like his sister.

"Do you think it's healthy for you to be doing this?"

She rolled her eyes and laughed. "Yes. And lord, don't let Micah hear you say that. He's already being a bear, and I'm barely four months along."

Conner still couldn't believe she was pregnant. It was another sign that life moved on. It wasn't until today that he'd realized how much everyone in his life had continued on while he had stayed perfectly still.

"So, what are your plans while you're here?" she asked.

He shrugged. "Not sure. Jillian took me to the swap meet a couple of days ago, and I've been to the beach."

"Jillian?"

"My landlady and an old friend of my sister's. She owns a house on the other side of the island and rents out the top floor of it."

"Ah. That's good. A lot of people don't take the time to get out of Honolulu except for part of a day. Where is the house located?"

"Near Kaneohe."

"Oh, we'll have to have you over for a meal. We live over there. You can bring your lady friend."

"She's not my lady friend."

Her eyebrow went up at his tone. "Okay. Micah will be down in a sec. He's talking to someone who's going to do research here."

"Does he do that often?" he asked.

Dee shook her head. "He told me this was a favor for a friend." Something caught her eye over his shoulder on the monitors, and her gaze softened. He turned and looked at the screens. Micah was walking with Jillian.

"What's she doing here?"

Dee stepped up beside him. "Her?"

"Jillian, why is she here?"

He felt Dee's study as he stared at the screen, but for a moment, he ignored it. He watched as Micah guided Jillian through the club, introducing her to people, some of them damned near half naked.

"Conner?"

"What?"

The silence that followed told him that Dee had not been happy with his tone. He glanced at her, and she was studying him as if there was something wrong with him.

"Jillian, she's your landlady?"

He nodded.

"So she's a writer?"

He nodded again as he looked back at the screen. He was fine until some jean-clad man with light hair and a cocky grin ran his finger down her arm.

"I think that's enough of that."

"Conner."

But he ignored Dee. He walked down the stairs to the floor and didn't slow until he got to their table.

Micah smiled at him, but Conner was ready to punch him.

"Conner, it's great to see you here."

Jillian spun around. "Conner? I thought you were going to see some old friends."

"I am. Dee, and to a point, Micah."

"Gee, thanks, Dillon," Micah said, but there was a thick thread of humor in his voice.

"What the holy hell are you doing here?"

She blinked at him, and he didn't blame her. His tone was proprietary, as if she had to answer to him.

"I'm researching."

"Is that what they call it now?"

She frowned at him and her eyes narrowed, but before she could say anything, the man who had touched her opened his big damned mouth.

"I've never known a man who's won a fight with a woman, mate. You might want to step back."

He glanced around Jillian and gave the man a nasty look, but his smile just widened.

"Elias St John, meet an old friend of the family, on Dee's side of course, former-agent Conner Dillon."

His eyes widened. "Dillon Securities?"

He nodded.

"Great operation you have there. I might want to talk to you about some security over at my ranch."

"I'm not licensed to work in Australia."

He laughed. "No, I own a ranch on the Big Island."

He dismissed the cocky bastard and studied Jillian. She had put on some makeup, and she had some kind of sparkly earrings dangling from her ears. Dammit. Noticing them made him think of just where else she might be pierced. It had been driving him crazy for days.

"What I would like to know is what you are doing here?"

She looked ready to hit him. "I don't think I have to answer any questions."

He knew he was acting out of character, and he didn't have a right to do what he was doing.

"No, you don't. You just didn't tell me you were coming here."

He heard a snort, and he was sure it was Micah.

"First, you didn't ask. Second, I don't think I have to clear my schedule with you."

He frowned at her, but she ignored him. Dee stepped up beside him. He glanced at her, but Dee wasn't paying attention to him. She was smiling at Jillian.

"Hi," Dee said, throwing him an amused look.

"I take it that you're Dee?" Jillian asked.

She had dismissed him. Something close to irritation, with a dose of possessiveness, moved through him. Conner didn't like it one bit. He knew he was attracted to her, even entertained the idea of an affair, but he rarely got jealous over lovers. Not since he was a teenager had he felt the need to gain a woman's attention. He didn't like it one bit.

Apparently, Dee picked up on his feelings because she gave him a smile before turning to face Jillian.

"Yes, I am. I take it you're the writer?" Dee asked. There was more than a little humor in her voice.

Jillian nodded, but before she could say anything else, St John muscled his way into the conversation.

"A writer?" St John asked. "What kind of writer?"

The suspicion in his tone caught Conner's attention. He studied the alertness in the man, the way St John now looked to be accessing Jillian in a way that had nothing to do with sex.

It was so subtle that most people wouldn't pick up on it, but Conner's years of training taught him to pay attention to the small cues.

"Romance, mainly erotic romance."

"Ah," was all the Aussie said for a moment and seemed to relax. "Romance, you say?"

Conner had heard the tone before from people. He hadn't spent much time until recently with Jillian, but he knew the way her back straightened that St John was in trouble. Maura had said that Jillian hated to be hit on because she was a romance author. Men seemed to think she was easy because of her genre.

"Do you ever do any hands-on research?"

She turned to say something horrible, which would probably leave the man in a fetal position on the floor, but someone called Conner's name. Loudly.

"Conner Dillon?"

He turned and found one of his old FBI friends, Maria Callahan, rushing toward him. She practically jumped into his arms.

A serious-looking man dressed in a suit came walking up behind her.

"I think you've stunned the man, Maria," the man said, but she paid him no heed. Instead she gave Conner a sisterly kiss on the cheek.

She stepped back with a laugh. "Oh, Rome, get over yourself. This is Conner Dillon."

"Yeah, I heard you scream his name like a little school girl and run over to jump him."

She rolled her eyes and smiled at Conner. "How are you doing?"

"I think you need to introduce me to the man who's planning on ripping my arms out of the sockets and beating me with them."

She laughed. "This is my fiancé, Rome Carino. Rome, this is Conner. My dad trained him, then he trained me. Dad sort of saw him as an honorary Callahan."

He offered a hand, and Carino took it.

"Wait, you said fiancé?" he asked, his brain still not functioning fully.

"Yes, it's a bit disgusting. Marriages popping out all over this club," St John said. "I'm going to escape before I get some of the 'get married' stench on me."

Maria smiled at him. "Eli, one of these days some woman is going to wrap you around her finger."

"What a pleasant idea," he said sarcastically. He gave Maria a kiss on the cheek that earned a growl from Rome, but the cowboy ignored it and walked away.

"I don't trust him," Rome said.

"You don't trust any man around me," Maria said.

"I have to agree with him," Conner said.

She gave Conner a look that told him that he would be better off staying out of the argument. "What are you doing here? I had no idea you were a member."

"Neither did I," Jillian said.

Maria peeked over his shoulder and smiled.

"Hi," Maria said and slipped past him before he could stop her. "I'm Maria Callahan. I knew Conner at the FBI."

Jillian smiled. "Nice to meet you. You know Eli?"

Maria chuckled. "At one time I thought he might be a serial killer."

Jillian glanced at the cowboy. "I'm assuming he was cleared?"

Maria nodded. "I have a feeling he might be guilty of something, but it wasn't of being a serial killer."

And knowing Maria, there was more to it than she was saying. Conner filed that information away to ask her about later.

"You say you worked with Conner? You look really young to be a contemporary of his."

Micah snorted, and Conner shot him a look.

"Her father trained me, and I helped train Maria."

Jillian's eyes were twinkling, her dimples starting to appear. His heart raced, and he had the sudden urge to kiss that smirk off her face.

"Oh, that explains it, because you are a bit older," she said.

"Hey."

She smiled at him and turned back to Maria. "Are you here with the FBI?"

Maria shook her head. "No. I left the FBI a few months back. I'm trying my hand at writing. I'm working on my first book."

Without missing a beat, Jillian slipped her hand into the back pocket of her jeans and pulled out a business card, handing it over to Maria. "Give me a call."

Maria's eyes widened when she saw the name. "Oh, thank you."

"So, what are your plans while you're here, Con?" Dee asked.

Everyone turned to him as if waiting to hear exactly what he said. He had never been under this much scrutiny in his life, and it was weird. "Just to relax."

There was a moment of silence then everyone who knew him started laughing.

"What are you laughing at?" Rome asked.

Maria shook her head. "You have to understand. Conner doesn't know how to relax. My father used to call him the Energizer Bunny."

"Well, thanks for that. What I want to hear is that my mentor compared me to a fluffy bunny," Conner said, only half joking.

"She's right, you know. There was some speculation in the dorm about that stamina," Jillian said.

He could feel heat singe his cheeks. "What the hell is that supposed to mean?"

She shrugged and blinked a few times in mock innocence. She opened her mouth to respond, but instead of keeping the conversation going, he grabbed her hand and tugged her to the dance floor.

She was laughing when he pulled her into his arms.

"Why, Agent Dillon, you're so forceful," she said, injecting more of her southern accent.

"You better behave yourself or you'll find out just how forceful I can get."

"I haven't said I have a problem with that."

Just hearing her say that had his body reacting. From the moment he had seen her in the club, he had wanted to touch her. Now he was getting to, but they were wearing too many clothes. And there were in public. She shifted against him, and he groaned.

She looked up at him with wide eyes. "What?"

"I'm riding a very fine line of control, Jillian." He bit out every word, trying to keep his irritation under control. He wasn't used to this problem. There had been women he had wanted before, but not with this force. That alone was unsettling and irritating. But the feelings of jealousy that had him melting down earlier were not common or welcomed.

She rose to her tiptoes and said, her breath feathering against his ear, "I promise I'm not trying to push it, but I have to admit, seeing you lose control might be fun."

She slipped back down off her toes, and he looked at her. She was, as always, honest with her feelings. In all the years he had known her, she had never tried to pretend or put on airs.

"I'll give you a warning. Behave yourself or you won't see anything of the club after now. Unless you're into public submission."

She shivered against him, and he groaned again.

"Please stop that."

"Sorry. When you say things like that, I can't help but be turned on."

He sighed. "This is going to be one long freaking night."

Jillian's body was still humming when she slipped out of her car a couple of hours later. Conner pulled his rental beside her and unfolded his length.

"Do you always drive so fast?" he asked.

She smiled at him, liking this version of Conner better than the FBI agent she knew, or the man who had shown up just a few days earlier. There was still that air of danger around him. There was no way he could diminish it. This was a danger of another sort, and it had anticipation dancing over her nerve endings.

"I like it fast."

There was very little light, but she could see the change in his expression. "Really," he said, his voice smoothing over the word and sending small sparks of excitement racing through her blood.

She had been right. He had been flirting with her. That thought made most of her brain melt on the spot. When she finally gathered her brain cells to answer, he had moved closer, resting his hand on her car behind her. She could smell him, that musky scent of his aftershave and...Conner. It took all her control not to lean in and sniff him.

"Yeah. But then, I know just how fast to go."

His expression hardened and even in the dim light, she could see the flush on his cheeks. Knowing she was getting to him had her libido revving.

"Do you know what you're messing with?"

She stepped closer. "I think that's who, not what."

His mouth curved. He slipped his hand around her waist, pulled her close, and kissed her.

At first gentle, then he deepened it, plunging his tongue between her lips. Everything in her yearned, wanted, needed. This man had been hitting all the points for days, and now she wanted him.

He moved and pressed his body against her. She would have to be dead not to feel his erection.

By the time he pulled back, her head was spinning and her heart was beating so hard, she thought she might pass out. Lord, the man was deadly with his mouth.

"Answer me one question?"

She couldn't seem to open her eyes.

"Jillian, open your eyes." When she didn't respond, he snapped out, "Now."

She did as he ordered before she even thought about it.

"Were you at Rough 'n Ready for fun or was it really research for a book?"

She smiled, knowing it would irritate him. She wanted to push him just to see his reaction and what it would do to her. "A little of both."

He didn't like that answer. She could tell by the way his eyes narrowed as he studied her. "I don't think you know what you're getting yourself into."

"Why don't you tell me about it, Conner."

She heard the challenge in her voice, knew that she was definitely hitting some hot buttons for him.

He crowded her against her car. The heat of him surrounded her, and she wanted another kiss. Another taste of the paradise she knew he would be able to offer her. Conner leaned down.

When his mouth was within a centimeter of hers, he said, "When you want to do more than play games, you let me know, Jillian."

Then, without kissing her, he pulled back and motioned toward her front door. For a moment, she couldn't gather her thoughts enough to walk. Her entire body was a throbbing hormone, and he had just stepped back and away from her as if it was no big deal.

She looked at him, saw the grim expression on his face, and realized that it wasn't easier for him than for her. She walked to her door. Conner took the keys from her and unlocked it.

She stepped inside and turned to face him. "You could come in tonight."

"I could, but you aren't sure. I want you to be sure. You know what I'm asking, right?"

She knew enough about BDSM to know he was asking if she was ready to submit. Something in her melted at the idea. She knew that Conner would definitely be a strong Dom. He might have had the air knocked out of him, but he was coming back to life. And with that, a man who needed someone to submit to him.

"Yes."

"Shut the door and lock it."

She did it without thinking.

"Good night, Jillian," he said through the door. Then, she heard his feet going up the stairs to his apartment. With a sigh, she dropped her purse and decided to get comfy and write. The man had definitely left her in a quivering mass of need, and it wasn't very nice of him. She undressed, and then tugged on a pair of knit shorts and a tank top.

Maybe she should take a cold shower. That might help her. Then, she collapsed on the bed. An ache for him welled up inside of her. Damn Conner for being such a good guy. A bad guy would probably have taken her up on the offer. But, of course, that was why she probably wanted to try this with him. She trusted him.

Knowing that didn't help her now. She needed relief. With a groan, she rolled over and opened the drawer to her night-stand. She was dipping her hand into it when she heard her cell phone ring. When she saw Conner's number, she wanted to groan again.

"Yes?"

"Don't even think about masturbating."

She froze. "You can see me?"

"No, but if you want to submit, you will not get yourself off tonight. You don't come unless I give you the approval."

She didn't want to admit it, but that turned her on even more. Damn, her nipples were so fucking hard they hurt.

"Jillian?"

She glanced at her drawer, at the big purple vibrator, and knew it would allow her to gain some relief and actually get some sleep.

"Don't."

That one word kept her from reaching for the item. With a sigh, she fell back on the bed.

"Now I'm not going to get any sleep."

"Learning the pleasure of restraint and enjoying the antici-pation will make the end more satisfying." He waited for a moment then said, "Good night."

He hung up without waiting for an answer. Her body was throbbing, wanting relief, but if he wanted to play this game, she would go along with him. She knew in the end he would make it worth the wait.

With that, she stood and pulled off her clothes. She needed a cold shower if she had any hopes of sleeping that night.

Jillian cursed when the family cell played Beethoven's Fifth for the third time that morning. Fate was definitely a bitch with a wicked sense of humor for giving her relations who were such a pain in the ass.

With her eyes closed, she reached for the phone and answered the call.

"Morning."

There was silence at first, then an aggravated sigh. "Really, Jillian, it's the middle of the afternoon. Are you still in bed?" her Aunt Blanche asked, her tone dripping with the disapproval it always did.

"How do you know I'm in bed?"

"You sound half asleep and you haven't answered my other calls."

"Maybe I was just ignoring them."

"Don't even try to lie to me. You were always lazing around in bed when you were younger. I don't know why it would be different now."

Most of the time, Jillian could be nice, but this time, she

was tired. She'd had little sleep after that hot kiss, knowing only a floor separated her from Conner. Not to mention she was beyond sexually frustrated.

"First of all, I don't need your approval for when I get out of bed. It's one of the reasons I don't live in Atlanta. I picked here to live because no one here gives a shit when you get out of bed."

"Language," her aunt admonished. The damned woman thought she had a right to tell Jillian what to do even thousands of miles away.

"You woke me up. You get what you get."

"If you would tell me where you lived, this would not be a problem."

No fucking way. If they knew where she lived, they would be popping up here looking for handouts. It was one reason she'd moved away from the mainland.

"Jillian?"

Jillian sighed. "What do you want?"

Blanche didn't say anything for a moment. Jillian knew what was coming. The family only called her for two things: death and money.

"Money. I've run low this month and need a little bit more."

It was only the fifteenth and she was broke. How did people go through ten thousand dollars in fifteen days? She lived in the family mansion, had her food provided, and not to mention, they didn't pay for utilities or their cars. Her grandmother was probably rolling over in her grave. But then she had made them all dependent on her while she had been alive, so it was really her fault.

"We talked about this. You have a set limit, as does Brent.

71

Charles already said no."

"Of course. Not all of us have all that extra money you have, and we have to survive. Lord knows you probably have a mansion wherever you live."

Jillian opened one eye and looked at her simple house, then shut it. Her house probably would fit into one of their bedroom suites.

"Sure, living in the lap of luxury. If it truly is for you, contact Charles and get an advance."

"I don't want that. This is an important living expense I need."

Which meant that her cousin Brent was still begging his mama for money. On top of that, he'd asked twice in less than a week, and he had been a coward and had his mother call her. He blew through the ten grand he was given each month like it was nothing. He had no living expenses since he lived with the rest of the family in a massive mansion outside of Atlanta. His ten thousand a month was for fun. And he couldn't seem to keep hold of it.

"Tell Brent to talk to Charles."

Her aunt paused. "He's in trouble. He had an accident, and now he needs a new yacht."

Jillian held the phone out and looked at it and then pulled it back to her ear. "So, this isn't anything other than Brent screwing something else up, and he ran to his mommy to fix it? Charles refused, I take it."

"Yes, he said that Brent could wait a few days to get money."

Jillian sighed. She needed the entire story, but she wasn't going to get it from her aunt.

"I'll call Charles and talk to him."

"Thank you. It is the least you can do."

Other than run the business and act as a nursemaid for a family of lazy idiots who always expected her to fix things, she did nothing in their eyes. She had a feeling that if she lived on the mainland, she would have to take sedatives to deal with them. Especially if they found out where she lived again.

"I have to go."

"Make sure you think about coming home for the annual deb ball. You know they would love to have you there."

Yeah, they loved their token. "Busy. I'll have Charles call you."

She hung up and rubbed her temples. She was getting a headache and it wasn't even noon.

The worries of her family dissolved when she heard a foot-step on her ceiling. So, Conner was up. Damn man kept her up most of the night. He had known when he told her not to touch herself that she wouldn't. He had known she would dream about it, too. How could she not? He was on her mind, driving her insane, and without a problem her subconscious had brought to life a totally delicious dream.

Her aunt had ruined it, though. Hearing that bitchy voice first thing in the morning was enough to make Jillian not want to think about men. As soon as she thought it, the image of Conner flashed through her mind. Okay, she could, and she could also melt at the idea. Just one little taste of him hadn't been enough. That much she knew. And the wonderful dream where he had her strapped to the bed had been ruined all because of her damned aunt.

With a sigh, she opened her eyes and hit Charles's number, knowing it was going to be all bad news. Better to get it over with because she knew from prior experience with her family that they were like a venereal disease. Ignoring them just made the problem worse.

***

"So, you liked Rough 'n Ready?" his sister asked. Conner sighed and regretted he had told her he had gone to see Dee.

"Yes, it was nice."

"I do like that club, and we are really lucky you are such good friends with the owner."

It wasn't that he was a good friend of Micah's, but he didn't point that out. His sister would just argue with him about that. Hell, he was pretty sure Micah would probably argue with him. He'd noticed that Micah seemed to adopt people into what he considered his family. Conner had a feeling that he and Maura were already considered family.

"So, whatcha doing today?" she asked.

He settled down in a chair and realized she wasn't going to let this go. With Maura, it was best to let her gnaw on whatever bone was bothering her at the time. "Not sure. Taking it easy."

There was a beat of silence. "Now you're scaring me."

He laughed. "No, it's just that I haven't talked to Jillian, who apparently thinks she is my personal tour guide. I also want to head on over to Bellows today."

Micah had told him it was a good place to boogie board, and it was a cool, windy day.

"Oh, well, if I know her, she's still in bed."

If he had been downstairs, she would definitely be in bed—beneath him.

Damn, he had to stop thinking about that. Just that little kiss had him wanting more, wanting her every way he could think of. Right now, he could imagine her on her hands and knees, that luscious ass of hers up in the air as he smacked it until it was red.

Shit. He was doing it again. And he was on the phone with his sister. Conner knew it was inappropriate, but even his silent admonitions didn't seem to quell his desire. He wanted her. Hell, even that was an understatement. He needed her in a way that was starting to worry him. He hadn't even touched her past that simple kiss, and he couldn't get her out of his mind.

"Conner?"

"Oh, sorry. What did you say?"

"I said that I bet she's still in bed."

"I heard her moving around a few minutes ago."

"Oh, well, she might be stuck."

"What do you mean stuck?"

"On writing. When she starts a new book, she tends to take forever. Usually, she finds some kind of distraction. A guy. Hey, is that Mick guy still there?"

"Yeah. Why?"

"I always thought they would hook up."

Just the thought had him fighting back a growl. As long as he was there, that motorcycle-driving idiot wasn't going to touch her. She was his.

That thought stopped him cold. Dammit. There he went again. The woman was driving him crazy. He had thought to keep his distance. He knew that was impossible after last night. He had proven that by taking the step and giving her an order. He would have never done that if he hadn't made the decision.

Conner didn't play fast and loose with his sexuality. He didn't mind a good healthy flirting session, but when it came to taking that next step, he never took it easily. It was probably one of the reason he hadn't had a long relationship in the last few years. He hadn't trusted any woman enough, or maybe he had sensed they didn't trust him.

"Conner?"

He realized he'd drifted off again. It was embarrassing how often he did that when it came to Jillian.

"I said I heard her moving around earlier."

"Not a good sign. Either she got more edits, which means you want to stay away from her, or she had to deal with her family."

"Deal with her family?"

"I'm not sure just what goes on with them, but I do know that about this time of the month, she gets a lot of phone calls."

He tucked that bit of information away to think about later. He heard her outside talking to Mick, and he wanted to see her. He knew one way to get his sister off the phone.

"So, what's going on with that Demeter case?"

"Oh, no you don't. The doc said only if we needed some kind of answer from you because of legal reasons. Otherwise, no dice."

"Okay. But, if you need me..."

"Forget it. I am not even in the mood to fight with you. Go find Jillian, go to Bellows. Have fun."

After hanging up, he wandered to the window and looked down on the scene beneath him. Mick was showing Jillian a tattoo, and from the looks of it, it was new. She didn't look happy at all, but she was faking it. He apparently asked her to go for a ride, but she shook her head. Conner could tell something was wrong. Even if she wasn't interested, Jillian was polite. Now she wasn't smiling, and there was an air of preoccupation about her.

She watched as Mick drove off, and then she started to walk back to the house. Conner knew this was the only way he could look casual, so he slipped out the door and down the stairs to the ground floor, catching her before she could escape into her part of the house.

"Hey, I was thinking of going to Bellows today."

"Sounds good for you."

Definitely not the attitude he was used to from Jillian. Could it be she was irritated with him from last night? Embarrassed? That didn't fit Jillian's personality. He couldn't remember a woman who was as straightforward about sex as she was. That was saying a lot considering he used to train Dommes. Add in a sister who'd felt the need to share way too much about her life when she was a teenager, and he was pretty accustomed to women being too open with him.

Jillian didn't hide anything. Or, in the short time he had spent in Hawaii, he thought she didn't hide things. She always seemed open and willing to share. Until now. Now, though, she was closed off.

"Not in a good mood today?"

She slanted him a look. "I needed about four hours more sleep."

He held his hands up. "You can't blame that on me. I stayed upstairs and out of your way."

She shook her head. "Not really."

"What do you mean by that?" he asked.

"Never mind. It isn't important."

"No, I think it is," he said, irritated with her now. She avoided looking at him, and it was really starting to bug him. "I can't believe you're upset about a simple kiss."

He saw her lips curve before she turned to face him. It did

things to him he didn't want to think about. The idea that a woman's smile, no matter how small, had his heart squeezing tight was not something he was used to. Allowing a woman to have that much power over him was a dangerous proposition.

She looked at him then, her eyes less troubled. He saw her brow ease, and again, he felt that little squeeze. Damn. Definitely not a good sign. Still, he couldn't help it.

She shook her head again. "There was nothing simple about that kiss, Agent Dillon."

"I'm not an agent," he said automatically.

She laughed. "Come on, let me have a little fantasy about you and winning the bet."

"Bet?"

"Yeah. We not only were preoccupied with you in college, but there was a bet going on about who would get the first kiss. Since I am assuming you never kissed any of the other dorm occupants, I think I won that bet last night."

Something loosened in his chest. He hadn't realized how worried he had been about her reaction to his kiss the night before.

"And the phone call after? Did you heed my instructions?"

The air stilled between them, the tension rising to another level.

"Why don't you come to Bellows with me today? There's some shade, right? You could settle there, take a nap while I play with my boogie board?"

She snorted. "Are you allowed to do that in public?"

He rolled his eyes. "Twenty minutes?"

Her cell phone went off, and her smile faded. "Give me thirty."

He nodded as she answered her phone. "Yes, Charles, I hear there's a problem."

He watched as she walked back to her front door. He couldn't get much from her side of the conversation, but he was going to definitely find out who Charles was and why he made her so fucking unhappy.

Jillian sighed with pleasure as she shifted on her towel. Conner was right. Going out was a good idea, and here in Bellows, there was spotty cell phone service, so she could ignore the phone calls. After her phone call with her aunt, she was happy to ignore them all. Charles's information was exactly what she'd expected. Yes, her cousins didn't know how to budget their money, and that was one reason her bitch of a grandmother left her in charge.

She brushed that aside and mulled Brent's problems. He had gone over the edge now, and there wasn't much that could be done about it. Charles had been blunt. His gambling problem had gotten out of hand. Worse, he had borrowed money from his mother. Money she would never see again. Jillian tried not to worry about that, knew that she had been saddled with the family money for one reason. So that her grandmother could have the last laugh.

She shook away those worries and looked out on the water. It wasn't that busy today because it was cool, with a little rain on and off, and it was the middle of the week. But there was Conner boogie boarding.

She watched as he crested over one wave and tried to ignore the way her body reacted. She had never been a woman who suppressed her feelings. Not anymore. Not since that bitch of a grandmother called her a nappy-headed loser. Still, there was something about Conner that warned her to be cautious. She had always thought he was the Alpha Dog of any group of men, but seeing him in the club last night—not to mention that kiss —she now knew Conner Dillon was definitely a Dom she could not take lightly.

He rose out of the water, and she sucked in a breath. For a man who just had a heart issue and was within spitting distance of forty, he was in fantastic shape. Hell, he would be considered in fantastic shape for a man in his twenties. Although, a man in his twenties wouldn't have that solid frame an older man did.

She watched as he walked to her and tried very hard to look away. She was gaping, she knew, and she didn't know why. There were gorgeous, half-naked men aplenty in Hawaii. Mick and Adam were always half naked. Maybe it was because she was accustomed to seeing him in suits.

Water sluiced down over his flesh, and she had to lick her lips. His muscled chest had a smattering of hair that formed a line that traveled down his stomach. It bisected a set of abs that would make a younger man look amazing.

"Gonna get out on the water?" He asked as he bent over to pick up his towel. The scent of the water was on him, the salt and sweetness of the Pacific clinging to him.

She cleared her throat as she tried to clear her mind and calm her libido.

"No, I'll just enjoy your attempts."

He dropped down beside her. "My attempts?"

"I'm sitting here wondering just how you know how to boogie board so well."

One eyebrow rose. "I do live in Miami."

"And you work seventy hours a week."

He shot her a smile, and she felt her heart turn over. Shit. He rarely smiled but when he did, he had full-on dimples. It almost made him look too pretty, if he hadn't broken his nose one too many times.

"I grew up in Florida too, remember. I did my fair share of surfing and boogie boarding. I wasn't that much into surfing. Like to ski, too."

She heard the wistfulness in his voice, and it would be easy to brush it away, but something told her to pursue it.

"You miss it."

He glanced at her then looked back out at the water. "A bit. I thought moving to Miami would give me more time on the water. Then, I got busy."

He didn't have to say with what. She knew as well as he did that Maura became the focus of his world when their parents died. A lesser man could have walked away. They had some distant relatives, but he didn't. And for someone like Jillian, who lost her parents at a young age, that made him even more appealing. She had spent her teenage years surrounded by men who spent their lives avoiding reality and responsibility. This made Conner all that more irresistible. Add in the dreamy body and those bedroom eyes, and she knew he was going to be trouble for her.

"So, how is the opening in DC going?"

He shrugged, and she couldn't help but watch the play of muscles. There was nothing like a great set of shoulders.

"Okay. I have a lot of connections there still."

"Like Maria Callahan from last night?"

He nodded. "Although, before last night, I hadn't heard she'd left the agency."

She laughed. "You act like she should have cleared it through you."

He gave her a glance then looked back out at the water. "No. I was her mentor until I left, and we kept up with each other until a couple of years ago. But, her father was Big John Callahan. It really is amazing that she left. I thought she would make a career out of it."

"So you think she was suited to it, like you were?"

He shook his head. "No, actually I was pretty sure that she hated it. Her father pushed her into it a bit. I remember being on cases and this teenager would be there hanging on his every word. She absorbed everything. It wasn't a normal childhood, and not once can I remember her ever being happy."

"She went on cases with him?"

He nodded.

"That is so many ways wrong."

Conner sighed. "I agree. It was unhealthy to the extreme. She learned that the only thing her father valued was catching a killer. So, I guess she thought that was the only way she would at least gain some satisfaction. She was a damned good agent, but I don't know if she ever liked it." He shook his head. "I would have never done that to Maura."

Of course he wouldn't. Conner had always tried his best to make sure Maura could live in a nurtured environment.

"Are you going to tell me what got you so upset this morning?"

She grimaced, and it was her turn to look away. "Family."

"I thought you didn't have much contact with them."

"As little as possible. I learned a long time ago that if I stayed out of their way, life was much easier. Of course, it would be better if I had picked a pseudonym to write under. They are still pissed that I use my real name."

"But you talked to someone this morning?"

She sighed as the memory of her conversations came back to her. "My aunt. She was trying to remind me of my obligations. I hate the word."

"Obligations?"

She nodded.

"Everyone has obligations."

Of course he would say that. He never shirked his duty, in work or home. Jillian was pretty sure that was one of the reasons he had never married. Conner was a man who stood by his word, and if he couldn't give himself to a woman one hundred percent, he wouldn't marry her. Why that made her sad she didn't know.

She shrugged. "In a way, yes. But these are the obligations that the poor relation has for the other people in my family, if you get my drift."

She felt his nod but couldn't look at him. Her family relations were so embarrassing. Jillian knew she wasn't responsible for their behavior, but it didn't make it any better. Conner took all his responsibilities seriously, more so than a lot of people. Knowing she was related by blood to some of the laziest, back-bitching jackasses in Atlanta society was humiliating.

"They aren't expecting you to come back to the mainland for something, are they?"

She glanced at him and realized he was really worried. She shook her head and chuckled. "Oh, God, no. They would rather have nothing to do with me, but they have some family issues, and they need approval from me on them. It was in my grand-mother's will, the old bitch."

"Do you think she might have been trying to keep you tied to your family for your own good?"

Jillian knew she could let him believe that. It wasn't like she hadn't done it before. Appearances had never been important to her, but getting into her family politics was not something she wanted to do with people. Even her lovers. Until now. He wasn't her lover yet, but she knew that it was going to happen without a doubt. For some reason, though, she knew she wanted him to comprehend just what she dealt with.

"You know the last thing she said to me?" she asked as she looked out over the water.

He shook his head.

"'It's too bad you've decided to take yourself down to your father's level. He was never good enough for my daughter. Blood will always tell.'"

He was quiet for a second or two, and then he said, "So your grandmother disapproved because he was a baseball player?"

She studied him for a second then realized that for Conner, he would never see her as her family did. "No. My father was black."

"Yeah, so?"

She smiled. "My mother's side of the family had old southern values, one of them being that you don't mix the races."

"But your mother didn't feel that way?"

She smiled then, remembering her mother and just how in love with her father she was. There was never a question in her mind. "Nope. And worse, she cut off all contact with her family. My grandmother actually tried to have my father arrested. It didn't work because Dad was the favored son of the Braves at the time."

"She tried to have Reggie Sawyer arrested?"

She laughed. "Yeah."

He was quiet for a second or two, then said, "You never talk about them much."

"Them?"

"Your parents. You complain about the Bentleys, but I never hear you talk much about your mother and father. I know you cared about them because you have pictures of them up in your house. The same ones you had when you were rooming with my sister."

The man never missed a beat. While it was aggravating that he noticed so much, it also gave her a sense of security in a way.

"It isn't like I lied about it. And after the accident, I hated people knowing. They always felt like they had to tell me they were sorry he died. So many people thought they knew him personally. It was kind of hard to take. And they always seem to forget I lost both my parents. It wasn't just my dad. Hearing the stories were the worst of it. It was a lot to take for a girl of ten. I guess an adult would have handled the grief better."

She didn't know if she would take it better now. Everyone felt that she should accept their grief, take it on, because for them she was the memory of her father. At the time, she had been overwhelmed by the attention.

He nodded in understanding. "Then you had to move in with your grandmother."

"I had no choice. She didn't particularly care for me or my father. She was still pretty mad at my mother for marrying him. Dad had only one brother. His parents died when I was just a baby, and the few extended family members he had were either too old or totally inappropriate to raise a child."

"Ah, yes, your uncle was Sam Sawyer, the football player."

"Yep. And he had a mean streak. Dad would never let me near him. So, off to grandmother's I went. And that whole crazy inbreed family."

He snorted out a laugh. "Inbreed?"

"They marry in their class, always white of course, and it is the same group of friends and acquaintances. You know there is some inbreeding going on there."

"So you have to stay in contact with them?"

She nodded but didn't want to go into her duties to the family. They just made her angry and sad. Knowing that the same blood that ran through them ran through her was embarrassing. She wanted to pretend that they didn't exist, at least for a little while.

"Since you got me out of my funk, why don't I treat you to lunch at Cholo's?"

"Not sure I like the sound of that."

She laughed, feeling better now that she had talked to him. "Fish tacos, bruddah. They are the best on the island."

He studied her for a second, then said, "You know, you don't have to be embarrassed about your family."

The fact that he could read her so well was a bit troubling.

Embarrassed? More like mortified, but she didn't like that he was so perceptive. "I never said anything about that."

"No, but I sense there are things you don't want to talk about because they're uncomfortable for you. I just want you to know that what your family does isn't about you. It's about them."

She could tell by the serious look in his eyes that he wasn't kidding.

"Thank you."

He slid his finger down her cheek and then traced her jaw.

Even though the sun was warm on her skin, she shivered. The breath tangled in her throat as he leaned forward and brushed his mouth over hers. She could taste the salt of the ocean on his lips, but he didn't deepen the kiss. Instead, he pulled back and smiled down at her.

"Fish tacos?"

It took her a few moments to get her brain to work. Her heart was still beating hard against her chest as her head spun. The man barely kissed her and she was melting there on the sand.

"Jillian?"

"Yeah, fish tacos. You'll love them."

"You lead, and I'll follow."

Conner glanced around the little restaurant. They had taken a seat outside, and he had enjoyed watching the mixture of tourists and locals mingle on the streets and the shops of Haleiwa.

Jillian made a humming sound, bringing his attention back to her. Again, Conner was amazed how much food Jillian could pack away. She ate like it might be her last meal, and he was pretty sure if he hadn't forgotten to eat breakfast, she would have outeaten him. He didn't know where she hid it. She wasn't slim, but she definitely wasn't fat. In fact, she was just the way he liked his women. He didn't like skin and bones. He liked a woman who didn't make him feel like a giant.

"Do you want another order?"

She laughed. "No. I think this was enough, although they are one of my favorite meals. I love the fish tacos here."

She took a sip of her drink and watched him over the rim of her cup.

"Thanks for pulling me out of the house today."

He started to wave it away, but she shook her head. "No, when I have to deal with my family, it can put me in a mood for days, sometimes a week. They aren't the most pleasant people to deal with."

"You have any cousins near your age?"

"A few. I wasn't ever that close to them. They saw me as an interloper."

"And, what do they do?"

Her brow furrowed. "Do?"

"Do, you know, for a living?"

She shrugged. "Most of them just live off the family money. Everyone gets a monthly stipend."

"But you work, so I assume that they must have to, also."

"I write, and I make a very nice living from it, but I don't have to work, if you get my drift."

"Really? So what do you do with all your money?"

She laughed. "That's really rude."

He felt his cheeks burning. "Sorry. It's just that your house isn't very high end. I like it, don't get me wrong, just that if you have that much money..."

"Why don't I have one of those palatial estates in Kailua or near Diamond Head?"

He nodded.

"First, that house is expensive because all land here on Oahu is. But I give to a lot of charities."

Of course she would.

"And you write so you can do that?"

"No, I can do that because I write. I don't choose to write."

"You have no control over what you do, is that what you're telling me?"

"It's been something that I have always wanted, but I don't truly choose to do it."

"Bullshit."

She smiled then and it reached her eyes. "It's the truth, I promise. That would drive you crazy, wouldn't it? I have a feeling you have control issues."

He shifted in his seat, ignoring her knowing look. It was one thing to live in the BDSM lifestyle. It was another thing for her to know it. If she knew it, his sister would, too. Maura knew of his lifestyle. He had never hidden it from her. It was different for his baby sister to know the dirty details.

"No comment?"

"Just because I know Micah and Dee doesn't mean I have anything to do with the club."

"I knew from the first time I met you that you had the tendencies of a Dom.

"You did not know I was a Dom the first time you met me."

"Okay, when I was in school, no. I didn't understand it then. But, I noticed how you would stride through those hallways like you owned the place. There was a reason there were always tons of girls with absolutely nothing to do the night you showed up to take Maura out."

"Now who's lying?"

"Seriously, you think a bunch of college coeds have nothing to do on a Saturday night?"

He had thought it odd, but he hadn't lived on campus when he went to school.

"Still, how would you know what I do in the bedroom by the way I act?"

She rolled her eyes in much the same way his sister did. But instead of irritating him like it did when Maura did it, it turned him on. Truth was, just about everything she did turned him on. Even when she was mocking him, he wanted her. It was like he was a teenager again with a crush.

He really was in deep.

"When you showed up here, I sensed it. I mean, I write the stuff." She shrugged. "And I have a degree in sociology with a minor in psychology."

"Lord."

"Why do all guys have that reaction?"

"Because women are always trying to figure out what makes men tick. With your degrees, there's a good chance you could figure it out and then tell us how to fix it."

Her lips curved as she leaned forward. "I would never use it to fix a man. Screw with his head, yes. Fix him, not my job."

He laughed, enjoying her sick sense of humor.

"You doubt me?" she asked.

He shook his head. "Not at all. I have a healthy degree of respect for a smart woman with your sense of humor."

"Good, you should know what you're getting into if you are thinking of messing with me."

"But you picked me out as a Dom even before I told you that day?"

She nodded to confirm his statement. "Like I said, with my background and, of course with my writing, I know the tendencies. If you hadn't told me, I would have definitely guessed after that kiss last night. If I didn't, calling me up and giving me orders went beyond just the normal phone sex."

She said it loud enough for the table next to them to notice.

"This is something you've done?" he asked.

Part of him wanted to know but another part of him didn't. He didn't want to think about her with another man. He had always thought she was a little dominant herself, but after last night, he wasn't so sure. She had always seemed so in control, so willing to take the reins.

"Dabbled. I have trust issues so that kind of lifestyle would be hard to deal with if I didn't trust the guy completely. Let's get back to you. Why don't you have a regular club back in Florida?"

His eyes narrowed. "Are you taking notes for your books?"

She chuckled. "No, but I will warn you that most things in my life have some kind of influence on my writing. Sometimes I don't even notice it until I read the final draft."

She shifted her braids over her shoulder, and it brought his attention to her tattoos.

"Rebellion?" he asked, nodding his head to her shoulder. She had a multitude of them, bright and colorful. He had never been into tattoos himself, but he had always had a secret thing for women who were. That and piercings.

"In a way. I am an expressive person. This is just another way of expressing myself. If I irritate the family in the process, so be it."

"I didn't think you saw them that much while you lived here."

"I don't, thank the good lord. Every now and then I do have to make it back to Atlanta for the quarterly business meetings. Plus, my PA lives there."

"Your PA?"

"Yeah, I hired a personal assistant. All my mail goes there, she sends it to me. And don't think that you got yourself off the hook. I still have a few more questions. So back to the club issue?"

"No. I tried out a few, but really didn't like them. I was a member in DC, had been a member of a club in Miami, but it closed down. After that, I just never found one that I liked."

"You like to do things in private? So you don't play in public?"

He shifted again but this time not from embarrassment. Just talking about this with Jillian was making him insane. He had wanted the woman before, but now he wasn't too sure of what he wanted from her. If she were a sub, it would add another level to their relationship he wasn't sure either of them were ready for. But, dammit, he wanted it. Wanted it so badly he was having trouble controlling himself. That hadn't happened in years.

"Depends. I tend to enjoy privacy more, but it isn't out of the question that I would go for fun and games at a club, especially when I was younger and wasn't in a long-term relationship. Plus, some subs have fantasies about submitting in public, or if I know it is something that will break them down...make them mine."

He saw the flare of interest in her eyes. It sparked something inside of him he hadn't felt in months, possibly years. He'd had relationships, and up until the last couple of months he'd had sex regularly, but he had grown bored with the scene, with the act. When he'd found himself going through the motions of a submission, he had decided to take a break.

Now, though, he was intrigued. If she had trust issues, she had probably never really submitted. Thinking of initiating Jillian into the lifestyle had his palms sweating and his cock standing at attention.

He realized she was staring at him as if trying to read his mind. "So you say you dabbled?"

She nodded and took a sip of her tea. It was easy to see the way her eyes had shied away for a moment, then rested back on him.

"A bit, but not with anyone in the lifestyle. I never took that leap."

"Why not?"

"I told you, trust issues."

Of course. He knew there was more than she was telling him. A woman with her family background would have some problems, but not to the extent he was thinking she might have.

"And last night was the first night you were at Rough 'n Ready?"

"Yeah. Your sister hooked me up because I want to write a suspense and there needs to be scenes in a BDSM club. I'd never been to one before."

That gave him pause. "Never?"

She shook her head. "I don't live the life. I do research, but this one actually has people working at the club, so I thought it would help. Micah was very accommodating."

"I just bet he was," he said. Even as he said it, he heard the irritation in his voice.

"Excuse me?"

He shook his head. He didn't know why he felt the spark of jealousy toward a man he considered a friend and who Conner knew was completely in love with his wife.

"I might have to interview that other Dom, though."

"Rome?"

She shook her head. "Well, wait, he might be good to interview, being a cop. But I was talking about the other guy."

She was starting to jump from one subject to the other, and his head was starting to spin. It was hard to keep up with what she was talking about.

"Who?"

"What? Oh, that Eli guy. And he's a cowboy from what the other women tell me, so that would be interesting."

"I heard that, but I would check his story again if I were you."

She gave him a knowing smile. "He lives on the Big Island. There are ranches there. There are even some here, too. Don't think you know everything about Hawaii until you've lived here for a while."

"I'm not going to live here."

She shook her head. "Of course not. Anyway, I need to get back and get some words on the page."

He didn't want to go, wanted to spend more time with her, but he knew better than to push.

"What?" she asked.

"Nothing."

"Okay, then, let's blow this joint. If I can get this stuff written, I get to watch shows tonight."

And he would have to find something to occupy his time rather than think about the woman who was, at this point, driving him over the edge.

Seven

Jillian couldn't write. The cursor was blinking on the screen, mocking her. For the first time in five years, she was sitting at her computer completely freaking out. She had never had a problem with writer's block. Okay, so at the beginning she sometimes had problems. It would go slowly or she would worry if she had the right idea about where the plot would go. Sure, she was more productive at other times than some, but she had always worked through it. She scoffed at people who said they had problems with it. It was easy to work through. She could jump onto something else...skip the scene that was giving her problems. As long as she kept moving forward, she was fine.

Now, she couldn't think of anything beyond the man upstairs.

The screen mocked her. Two hours. She hadn't written anything but two words in two hours. *Chapter One*. It was enough to give a girl a panic attack.

There had only been a couple of times she had issues, but as she had remembered, she had worked through them. Each time it had been her family problems getting in the way. She wished that were the case now. That would be easy enough to deal with. Her family issues were small compared to the person who was occupying her mind right now.

Just imagining him up there had her blood temperature soaring. That discussion at lunch had made her little crush even worse. Knowing for sure he lived in the lifestyle, seeing the way he watched her when they spoke—it had her insides going all flip-floppy on her. Jillian wasn't a woman who went gooey because a guy paid attention to her.

She closed her eyes and sighed. The man was going to kill her. Being in her house a month, knowing what he liked to do in bed...

Of course, she wondered about his preferences. She knew from research that Doms all had their own likes and dislikes. Was he a spanker? A little zing of heat pulsed through her blood at the thought. Did he like to use a paddle or a cat o' nine tails? She shifted in her chair and groaned when she felt her wet panties rub against her clit.

The man was driving her to distraction. What was she going to do about him? The normal Jillian would go for it and to hell with the consequences, but she had other concerns here. First and foremost, his sister was her friend. Maura was one of the few female friends Jillian had. She had been her best friend for years, and Jillian didn't want to ruin that. If the fling ended badly, she didn't want to lose Maura. And that is all it could be, a fling. She wasn't a woman for long relationships. Men tended to get in the way, and she had those trust issues.

Her other worry was meeting his needs in the bedroom. Would she be able to do the things he wanted, needed, from her? She wasn't sure she could, wasn't too sure that she wanted to.

Scratch that. She *did* want to—there was no doubt about that. She had always been intrigued by the lifestyle. It's how she'd started to write BDSM themed books. She had spent years researching, talking to subs and Doms. Sir Samson, the first Dom she'd interviewed, had told her that she was a submissive, but she wouldn't submit to just anyone. He claimed her trust issues would make it damned near impossible for anyone to get her submission. She should email him and tell him just what she was going through. Lord knew Sir Samson had a sick sense of humor, and he would surely appreciate her situation.

But she couldn't. This was private. And that told her that it was more than just a fling. Which scared the hell out of her. She wasn't emotionally equipped to handle a true relationship. She had proven that more than once. This time was different. Never before had she held back from Sir Samson, but now she was.

Why?

There was only one thing that would have her keep things from Sir Samson. Her heart was involved—and that scared the living shit out of her.

She had a healthy sex drive. She didn't sleep around, and she didn't believe in one-night stands. Still, she did keep her relationships light and easy. With Conner, there would be no light about it. They were tangled up in so many ways that she wasn't sure she could deal with it when it ended. And it would end. She would never move back to the mainland and he would never move here.

There was a knock at her door. Jillian was thankful and irritated with the interruption. She needed to stop mooning over Conner, but she wasn't quite ready to stop. With a sigh, she walked to the door wondering what Mick and Adam needed tonight. The two men never seemed to be able to make it to a grocery store.

She opened the door and found Conner Dillon standing on the other side of it, one shoulder propped up against the door-jamb. The sun was setting, slipping behind the mountains that were at his back. Every drop of moisture in her mouth dried up.

"Did you get your writing done?" he asked.

She sighed. He looked too good to ignore. How could a man wear a pair of shorts and T-shirt and seem to intrigue her in a way no other had before? She saw men half naked every day in Hawaii, but she was sure this one would catch her attention if he were dressed from head to toe. Part of it, she knew, was that she was accustomed to seeing him in more clothes. Now, though, he looked like a local...down to the bare feet.

"No."

"Oh, sorry, I guess I should let you get back to it."

But he didn't move. The sweet air thickened around them, the tension growing as it had the night before. Jillian knew she should tell him to go away. Playing the temperamental author was never that hard for her. She was a temperamental author and had used it to her advantage in the past. Now, though, she couldn't. She needed to spend time with him, wanted it with a scary type of lust that had her worried. Still, she pushed those thoughts aside.

"No, come in. I'm having a bad time writing, so I need a break."

She turned and walked toward the kitchen. She needed something cold to drink, and looking at him just made her want to jump his bones. Instead of gaining relief, she felt his gaze on her back. Shit. The door shut quietly, and his footsteps followed her.

"Do you normally have issues with writing?" he asked.

She shook her head as she pulled out a pitcher of strawberry lemonade she had made earlier. "Want some?"

For a moment, he just looked at her with those solemn eyes of his, and she felt her heart turn over. God, the man was wicked. Without a word, he had her. He didn't have to touch her, and she was ready to be naked. Now.

After another moment or two, he nodded.

Drawing in a deep breath, she set the pitcher down on the counter then grabbed a couple of glasses.

"What do you think is causing the issue?" he asked. His voice had deepened, vibrating over the words.

What the hell was he talking about? He expected her to carry on a conversation when he was looking at her like he knew what she looked like naked. She couldn't remember her last name.

"Issue?" she asked as she turned around and started to fuss with the drinks.

"With writing."

"Oh, the family crap. I'm sure it has driven me over the edge."

But even to her own ears it didn't sound believable.

"Really?" He didn't sound like he was buying her excuse. She wasn't buying it, so there was a good chance he wasn't either. He stepped behind her, resting his hands on the counter in front of her. He wasn't touching her, but he surrounded her. She felt the heat of his body, could smell the clean, crisp scent she always associated with him.

"Put the glasses down, Jillian."

He hadn't raised his voice. If anything, it lowered, deepening over the vowels. It sent another jolt of lust spiraling through her. Heat danced over her nerve endings.

"Do it."

For a second, she gripped the glasses tighter. She knew what he was asking. Part of her rebelled against the idea of doing what he ordered. Still, there was a part of her that wanted to do it, to please him. It scared her a bit—a lot. But she did as he ordered and set the glasses down.

"Put your hands on the counter for me."

Again, he didn't raise his voice. There was a thread of lust in his tone now, one she had heard last night when he called her. Without a thought, she did as he commanded. It was as if she couldn't think for herself, didn't want to. Her body was throbbing and he hadn't even touched her yet.

He inched in behind her, his chest against her back, his groin against her ass. His cock was hard, but he did nothing more than lean against her. The restraint was a power play. She understood that, and dammit, she responded to it. Her heart was racing, and she felt her body temperature soar. He covered her hands with his. When he spoke next, she felt his breath against her ear.

"You have two choices right now. You can tell me no and send me on my way. I will accept that. I won't be very happy because I have a need for you that is about to kill me, but I will accept that."

He would. She knew without a doubt he would walk away and allow her space. That made her want him even more.

"The second option?"

"I take you in your room and show you exactly what you're missing in the bedroom. You are a sub down to your toes, Jillian."

She straightened, and he chuckled.

"That doesn't mean anything against you—and you know that. It doesn't mean you aren't a strong woman. In fact, some of the strongest women I know are subs. What it means is you need something in the bedroom other men haven't been giving you. Considering what you write and how smart you are, you have to know that you're missing something."

She knew that, knew it in her heart. Every time she slept with a man, she was satisfied to a point. There was always something missing in the relationship. Was it this?

"So, tell me, Jillian, which one do you want? Do you want me to stay or leave? Understand, if I stay, you will go in that room and be under my control."

She swallowed. She knew what she wanted, what she yearned for. The kiss the night before had told her that, had let her know just what she was missing. His quiet control of things always set her off. He'd turned her on with the order last night on the phone more than any man who'd touched her.

"Jillian, tell me now or I will think you don't want me."

It would tangle them up good, and not just in bed. Her good sense told her to ignore the need he built in her, but she had never been really good at ignoring her needs. She sighed.

"Stay."

eight

Conner's heart was thudding so loudly, he was sure Jillian could hear it. He hadn't planned on this when he had stopped by. He had expected to just say "hey," and head out. That had been the plan. He didn't know where he had planned to go, but he had needed to get away. She might have shown some interest the night before, but Conner wanted to make sure she'd had time to think about what he expected from her in the bedroom. It wasn't something any person should take lightly, the Dom or the sub.

But she had been standing there, wearing a pair of cut-off jeans and a T-shirt, her frustration easy to see. He wanted to do anything he could to soothe the worries she had. It wasn't that common for him to care so damned much about making another person happy, but with Jillian, he did. If she had sounded more believable in her explanation of her writer's block, he knew he would have left. But the tension between them was too much to ignore.

He slid her braids aside, draping them over her shoulder, and nuzzled her neck. God, the woman smelled like sin. She was always warm, welcoming, and smelled of coconut and sin. How could any man resist her? He was amazed that she didn't have a string of men waiting outside to have her. But then, Jillian was pickier than most women he knew.

"Conner?"

For the first time in all the years he had known her, she sounded unsure of herself.

"What?"

She shivered, and he felt it to his core. Her generous ass moved against his cock, and he thought it was a good thing he was still dressed. Otherwise, he might not be able to control himself. Hell, he almost embarrassed himself and came right there. He couldn't remember wanting a woman this badly before.

"Shouldn't we move to the bedroom?" she asked. The uncertainty he heard in her voice tugged at emotions he usually tried to keep hidden.

He smiled against her hair. This was going to be the best time he'd had in years. She was always trying to control the situation, and he was going to enjoy breaking her of that habit.

"Let me worry about that. I'd like you to take your shirt off."

She hesitated.

"This isn't going to work if you ignore my commands."

He put enough steel in his voice to let her know that he wasn't fooling around with her.

She did as he ordered, and he sucked in a breath when all he saw was her bare flesh. The T-shirt she had been wearing was big, so he hadn't been sure if she was wearing a bra or not.

He spread his hands over her back, then moved her braids

over her shoulder once more. He kissed his way down her back, nipping at the flesh along her spine. She sighed.

"Your shorts."

She hesitated again. He let his lips curve slightly. Conner was ready for this challenge.

"I told you that you had to obey me. Do it now or I walk away."

She did, and it was his turn to sigh. The woman was wearing a thong. It was blue and showed off her ass perfectly. His cock twitched. Hell, his dick was throbbing, and he wondered if there was any blood in his brain. He bit back on the hunger now clawing at his stomach. This wasn't so much about him or his desires. He knew what he wanted in the bedroom. This was about Jillian finding out what she needed to be complete.

"Give me a word, one that will tell me that I have gone too far or that you have had enough."

"Chocolate," she said, her words coming out with a sigh of pleasure as he glided his hands over her ass.

So smooth, so right. He hoped she was into anal because he could think of nothing more than fucking that tight little hole until she came so many times she couldn't remember her name.

That would come later. Tonight, she needed to be taught a lesson—one that she would never forget if he did it right. He turned her in his arms and then lifted her onto the counter. Before she could think of closing her legs, he stepped between them.

God, she was perfect. Her breasts weren't overly large, but they were pert and so firm. He ran the backs of his knuckles over first one nipple then the other. Immediately they tightened. They were so fucking responsive.

He leaned down and took one into his mouth as he pinched the other. She threaded her fingers through his hair, but he pulled back and said, "Hands on the counter, Jillian."

The narrowed look she gave him almost had him laughing, but he said nothing as she did as he ordered.

"Good girl."

She opened her mouth to blast him, he was sure, for the girl comment, but he slipped his fingers between her legs and pressed. She shivered.

"You have to learn that was a compliment, and pretty soon, I can assure you, you will crave those words. You continue being good, and I will make sure you're rewarded."

She closed her eyes and moaned as he teased her a bit more, then took her nipple into his mouth again. He was fine until he felt the piercing on her clit. He closed his eyes and called on what little control he had, but it was hard to do that. He could imagine just what it looked like. Trying his best to forget the picture he had created in his head, he kissed his way down her body. He reached her belly button and slipped his tongue over her piercing there. Maybe it was because of the woman and her rebellion against her family, he wasn't sure. It represented a part of her personality that he loved. Either way, he liked it. In fact, he was definitely halfway to loving it. He loved seeing the metal shimmer against her skin.

He tasted her flesh, moving his mouth over her thighs, working his way to her pussy. He tapped the insides of her legs.

"Spread them."

She did this time with little hesitation. Her breathing was faster, and he watched as her breasts rose with each breath. *Damn*.

He went to his knees in front of her.

"Scoot up."

She did as he ordered again, apparently anticipating what he was going to do to her. Leaving the panties on, he set his mouth against her. He knew the added friction of the silky fabric would heighten her need. It would frustrate her. The barely-there panties would rub against her but not give her relief. Over and over, he used his tongue to shift the panties against her.

But soon, driving her crazy was driving him crazy. As he rose to his feet, Conner slipped his fingers beneath the fabric. He slipped the thong off and tossed it on the floor behind him.

He dropped to the floor again. His cock twitched as he saw the small gold ball on her clit. Fuck that was sexy. He placed a hand on each thigh and then set his mouth on her pussy. She was already wet, dripping with her need. The flavor of it exploded over his taste buds. Decadent—sweetness with a hint of spice. Dipping his tongue between her labia, he teased her clit and tugged her piercing between his teeth.

She was squirming against his mouth.

Soon she was moaning, and he could feel her approaching orgasm. He pulled away.

"Fuck."

He gently tapped her pussy. "Bad girl."

She frowned at him.

"First, no speaking unless I ask you a question or you're using your safe word. And *I* give you pleasure. *I* am in control of that just as I am in control of you. If you can't handle that, we need to stop right now."

He waited then asked, "Is that okay with you?"

She hesitated, and that worried him. He couldn't have her any other way. For the first time in years, he knew he couldn't deal with her any other way in bed. He needed her absolute submission.

Then, she looked him in the eye, her gaze steady as her lips curved slightly. "Yes."

Something in his chest loosened and filled him with warmth. It was beyond the heat of lust, but he wasn't ready to figure out what that meant. To either of them. Right now, all he wanted was her.

"Let's go."

He helped her off the counter and led her to the back of the house.

"Which room?"

"Last door on the left."

He stepped into the room and turned on the light. It was a lot like the woman herself. A mix match of items that shouldn't go together, but they did. He led her to the bed and sat her down. He was happy there wasn't a footboard. It gave him more possibilities.

She watched him, holding his gaze with a challenging one of her own. He knew there were Doms who didn't like that. They wanted a submissive to show it in every way. That just wasn't his thing. In fact, he found it even more arousing to have a woman who was strong, one who knew her own worth, yet allowed him complete command of her body and pleasure.

He couldn't fight the curving of his mouth as she continued and refused to look down. Good. It was the right start to this relationship.

Whoa, there. This wasn't a relationship. Not even the start of one. This was just...something. He pushed those thoughts aside.

"Do you have a scarf or something I can use?" he asked.

"For what?"

"You don't question me unless you want to stop."

Her lips twitched. "I mean, how long do you need? I have a bunch of different ones."

"Long."

"I have several longer ones in the top right-hand drawer of my dresser."

She stood up to get it, but he shot her a look that caused her to stop.

"I did not give you permission to move. Sit back down."

She frowned, but she did as ordered. He had a feeling that she didn't like anyone invading her privacy, but she was just going to have to get used to it with him in her life. In every aspect.

He opened the drawer and pulled out a long blue scarf. It reminded him of the waters in Kaneohe Bay. And Jillian.

He walked to her. "I'm going to tie this over your eyes. You're going to have to get used to my touch but also to giving over the control of your senses to me."

She nodded but said nothing. He smiled as he tied the silky material over her eyes. He knew she didn't like it. If he thought it pushed too many buttons, he wouldn't do it, but he could tell she wasn't scared. He removed his clothes and still said nothing. Then, he joined her on the bed.

"Lay back and roll over onto your stomach."

She did.

"Palms on the bed."

When he had her in the position he wanted her in, he took his sweet time looking at her.

Perfection. She was in good shape, yes, but not overly

skinny. He didn't go for skin and bones. Jillian had an abundance of succulent flesh.

"I put the blindfold on you so that you learn to feel. Just feel and enjoy."

He brushed aside her braids to look at the colorful ink on her shoulders. The tattoos were over her shoulders and then the snakes tangled together on her back. He skimmed his fingers down her spine, enjoying the way she shivered. She was already in tune with him on some level. He could just imagine the further they went just how she would react.

Without saying anything, he kissed his way down her spine. God, she was sinful. Even her flesh tasted of temptation. Sweet and tart and so like the woman he'd lusted for since he'd arrived. The scent of her rose from her skin, filling his senses, and his need spiked. It had been so long since he'd been able to enjoy a woman who engaged him on so many levels.

When he reached her ass, he slipped his fingers between her cheeks.

"Have you ever had anal sex?"

She paused, and when she still didn't answer, he smacked her ass. The sound of it, plus her indrawn breath, had him ready to come right there. He was thankful for the years he'd spent training to be a Dom because it was the only thing helping him hold onto his control. His hand stung from the slap.

"Yes. A few times."

Part of him was irritated because he would have liked to been the first, but the fact that she had made it easier for them to do that. But not tonight. Tonight he was going to fuck that tight little pussy.

He slid his mouth over her ass, nipping at the fullest part of it. She moaned and he did it again. The way she responded, he knew she was definitely ripe for a spanking. He wanted to rush, to turn her over and plunge into her core, feel her inner muscles contract while her wet heat surrounded him, but he needed to draw it out. He wanted her as on the edge as he was because he knew it would be more than either of them would ever forget.

He sat up and slapped her again. Over and over he smacked her and enjoyed the way with each slap, she squirmed or moaned.

Soon, his hand was as warm as her ass, so he pulled back. She was squirming on the bed, and without a doubt, ready to do anything to come.

"Turn over."

She did as ordered and he smiled—only because she wouldn't see it. She was ready to be his sub by her easy compliance when she wasn't thinking. She was already in tune with him.

When she lay back on the bed, he had to fight to keep his breathing steady.

The red silky sheets were another contradiction of the woman. One would expect that she would have something practical, because so much about her was practical. But like the tattoos or the braids, here she showed her inner self, the one who called to him on so many levels. She lay there completely nude, the red of the sheets the perfect backdrop for the work of art of her body.

He shook himself out of the daze he seemed to be in and moved up to the head of the bed. After removing the blindfold, he wrapped his hand around his cock, giving it one long stroke. Then, he said, "Take my cock in your mouth."

She didn't hesitate. With little preamble, she came up on her elbows and reached over to take him in. The first swipe of her tongue almost had him coming. She licked up and down the length of him, then swirled the tip of her tongue over the top.

"Stop fucking around."

She smiled up at him, and he knew she was doing just that. Or rather, fucking with him. She kept her eyes on his as she wrapped her mouth around his cock. He watched as each inch disappeared between her pink lips. Then, she started to move him in and out of her mouth. She slowly built up speed, using her tongue to drive him closer to the edge. She reached up and caressed his balls. He should reprimand her for doing something he didn't order, but fuck, it felt so good.

Soon, though, he felt his release nearing, and he wasn't ready. Beyond that, the woman needed to learn that he was the one in control of the situation, of their pleasure. He pulled away, and she frowned at him.

He grabbed the scarf. "Back down on the bed."

She apparently didn't like his tone. He didn't give a damn. He wanted her so fucking bad that he didn't care if he pissed her off. It was good because that meant he was doing his job as Dom.

"Do it now, or I walk away."

She apparently took his threat seriously because she lay back down on the bed.

He grabbed the scarf he had picked out. "Lift your arms up."

When she did, he tied her hands above her head and then secured the scarf to the slats in the headboard.

"Now, we'll see who's in charge," he murmured more to himself than to her. She showed no reaction at all. He didn't know if he liked that or not. He thought she might be a bit of a challenge, hoped for it actually.

Pushing those thoughts aside, he straddled her body.

With slow movements, he skimmed his hands over her breasts. She wasn't big on top, but he had never been a man who appreciated fake breasts. He liked them natural and small. He teased the nipples, happy with her indrawn breath when he pinched them. He bent his head and licked over first one, then the other nipple, then worked his way down her body again. He didn't think there had ever been a woman who had done this to him. Lord, the woman was a tasty treat. But he had the sense that she was holding back, trying to control the situation. So, he figured it was time to establish just who was in charge in bed.

He slipped between her legs and pushed them apart. She was turned on. The evidence glistened on her labia, and he knew she was barely holding on. But she was, and that didn't sit well with him.

He licked her, leisurely, enjoying the flavor of her again. Again and again he tasted her, skimming his tongue around her pussy lips. She started to squirm, but he paid no heed. As he had thought, she was under the assumption she could control the situation, and until she completely gave over to him, he would not be happy. He knew it wouldn't happen completely tonight, but now he was going to teach her a lesson.

Conner lifted his head and smiled up at her. "Now, you've been holding back."

She didn't say anything.

"And one thing I do is make sure a sub knows that I give her the pleasure. She has no control over her body in this bed other than to tell me I'm going too far. You always have the ability to tell me no."

He waited but she said nothing again, and he took that as assent.

"You've been trying to keep from coming, that I feel. Not that I had given you permission, but I could feel you doing it when I was eating your sweet pussy. And, one thing I will tell you is that you will pay dearly for that."

He smacked her pussy, and her eyes narrowed although she kept silent about it.

"That's good." He smacked her again. "You're going to learn that what I do to your body is out of your hands."

He gave her cunt another good lick then set his mouth on her again. This time, though, he was relentless. Over and over he dove into her hot core, swiping his tongue in and out and then over her clit. He knew it was driving her crazy because her legs were starting to move on the bed, but he ignored that. Instead, he pushed her further and further. Her first orgasm hit her hard as she bowed her body up off the mattress and screamed his name. He did not stop. Instead, he redoubled his efforts, taking her hard clit into his mouth and playing with her piercing. He rose up, slipping his hands beneath her ass and pulling her up with him.

Then, he slipped a finger between her cheeks, playing with her puckered opening. He could just imagine slipping into her ass, fucking her until both of them couldn't stand.

The image brought another drop of pre-come on his dick, but he ignored it. Conner continued his assault. Without pausing, he had her coming over and over, and when he was sure she'd finally learned her lesson, and when he wasn't sure he could control himself any more, he settled her back on the mattress. He grabbed the condom and ripped it open. She was watching him as he rolled it on.

He didn't want to wait, didn't think there was a reason now.

His hands were shaking when he lifted her and entered her in one swift thrust.

She sighed in pleasure as if she had been waiting for this all along. He tried to move slowly, but he soon felt the control slipping out of his hands as her muscles contracted over his cock. Every little ripple pulled him deeper. He thrust once, twice...then he came, his orgasm pulled from the deepest part of his soul.

He shouted her name as she came with him, her orgasm causing her muscles to contract harder on his shaft, milking his release, pulling him so deep into her hot, wet sex he shivered with the power of it.

When he was spent, he fell on top of her. She grunted in reaction.

"Sorry."

"What's there to be sorry about?" she asked, and he heard the smile in her voice.

He lifted his head and looked at her. Her eyes were closed, and she looked downright smug. Conner lifted his hands to untie her arms.

"Jillian, open your eyes."

She did slowly, and he had a feeling she was worried that by doing it, reality would be unpleasant. As if they were in a dream. He knew he felt that way. He had barely played with her, but this joining had been more powerful than with any sub, even his first.

"Thank you."

She smiled at him, and he leaned in for a kiss. Soft, slow, and filled with a tenderness that he didn't know he was capable of. It amazed him and stunned him how much he wanted to take care of her, to make sure she was nurtured and loved. It was something that had him frowning as she settled back down against her red pillows.

"Stop worrying."

He looked at her. 'What?"

"Stop worrying. You worry too much. Just sleep."

He shook his head and said, "You still think you can boss me around?"

"In this, I can. Let's get some rest."

He smiled as he lay down and pulled her into his arms. The woman had a lot to learn.

It was his last thought before falling asleep.

nine

The University of Georgia fight song sounded on her phone, and she groaned. Lord, she was tired, and she wanted to bury her head under the covers. She rolled over and found the spot empty. Opening one eye, she looked around for Conner but only found his side of the bed empty. She sat up, irritated that he had left without saying anything, but then she noticed his shirt on the chair beside her bed.

The ring started again, and she knew the only person under that ringtone was Maura.

"Hey, Maura. Kind of early for you to call."

"It's ten in the morning there, and I can't get ahold of Conner."

For a second, Jillian's brain just stopped working. It stuttered to a stop, and she couldn't seem to get it to function again.

"Jillian? Is everything all right?"

Maura was starting to panic. Jillian had heard it enough times to know what it sounded like.

"Maybe he's sleeping?"

"You know Conner. He doesn't sleep. Not this late."

116

"He's on vacation."

She caught a movement out of the corner of her eye and saw Conner standing there with nothing but the jean shorts he'd worn the night before. They were zipped but not buttoned. Lordy, talk about a mind melt. With the sun streaming in behind him, his skin looked almost golden. Men sucked because she knew she looked like crap. All they had to do was get up and they were sexy. His hair was a little mussed and she could imagine threading her hands through the strands, moving it this way and that.

"Jillian!"

"What? Oh, sorry. I was distracted."

His lips twitched as he folded his arms across his chest. The knowing look in his eyes told her he knew how he affected her. Damn the man. It irritated her that he accepted her attraction so easily. She probably looked like something the cat dragged in and here he was looking like a million bucks.

"You don't think anything has happened to him?" Maura asked, her voice filled with worry.

Jillian choked and then cleared her throat. "No, I think he's fine."

He rolled his eyes and walked forward. He took the phone from her.

"Hey, Maura. Is there a reason you need to get ahold of me? Just a reminder, the doc said not to bother me with work."

He smiled at his own joke, but listened. "Tell him he pays the retainer we asked for or we don't do the work."

Maura's voice sounded over the phone.

Conner shook his head. "I don't care. And he's fucking with you. He has plenty of money to pay for it. He just doesn't want to do it. He has always been cheap. Make sure he understands if he can't pay, we'll dump him. But don't say it like that. Be a little nice, but turn the screws."

Then Maura continued so apparently Conner thought it was a good time to sit down on the bed beside Jillian. He was smiling when he bent and brushed his mouth over hers. It wasn't even a kiss really. It was just a touch, done before she could even respond, but it had her body reacting nonetheless. He nuzzled her neck as Maura started asking questions about his night and why he hadn't answered his phone. She felt his tongue over her earlobe, then his teeth. She couldn't stop the hum that vibrated in her throat.

"I left it upstairs," he said, causing his breath to feather over her flesh. She shivered in reaction.

Another round of questions followed, and he sat up. Jillian could see that he was annoyed. She realized that answering to a younger sister, one who had to answer to him for most of her life, wasn't sitting well with him. "Listen, I came down last night to chat with Jillian. She jumped my bones and I completely forgot about my phone. Needless to say, she is ready to jump my bones again so I figure I should let you go."

Maura was squawking as he hung up. He tossed her phone on her bedside table.

She frowned at him. "Why did you tell her that?"

He shrugged. "It was true."

He moved to nuzzle her neck again. Her body started to heat, and God, she wanted that. She wanted nothing more than to forget about the phone call, but Maura was her best friend, and she didn't want to mess that up. She needed answers.

"Why did you tell her like that?"

"You did jump my bones," he said, his voice deepening. She could hear the arousal simmering, building.

"Good lord, a nice time to get a sense of humor, Conner."

"I've always had a sense of humor. I just kept it well hidden. In my line of business, you have to be careful who you trust."

She sighed as he nibbled on her ear. She wanted to discuss the issue of telling Maura, but he had a way of scrambling her brain. "Why did you get out of bed?"

"To cook you breakfast."

Her eyes shot open. "Sex and breakfast? You are a god."

He sat back and gave her a lopsided smile that had her heart turning cartwheels in her chest. "All women say that after a night with me."

Her throat was closing up at the sweetness of the man. He had given her one of the best nights of her life and here he was, treating her like a princess the next morning. Who would have known that Mr. Cold-Eyed FBI agent and security expert would be so sweet? And just how was she going to keep herself from falling in love with him?

She pushed that thought aside and concentrated on him. Living in the moment was something she had done for years and she could do without a thought now. Hopefully.

"Our waffles are going to get cold if I stay here much longer. Why don't you get dressed and join me out in the kitchen?"

She smiled and gave him a kiss. "You got it."

He left her then, and she felt comfortable rubbing her chest and trying to ease away the clutching of her heart. Lord, the man had been there a week and he was getting to her. She'd allowed him things that she had never allowed another man, and she wanted more. She knew if he asked for something, she would do it. As if he had heard her thoughts, he poked his head inside the door and said, "And make sure you wear a shirt, no panties."

With that he left as if knowing she would follow his orders. Of course she would. If he could repeat what he did to her, she would be happy to sit anywhere without her panties. He was hard to resist before, but now that he was being kind of adorable...no woman in her right mind would turn him away.

She slid out of bed and winced. She was in good shape, did yoga on a regular basis, and was pretty active living in Hawaii. But last night had shown her just how long her love life had been dormant. And even when she had gotten someone in her bed, apparently it hadn't been all that thrilling. She closed her eyes as she brushed her teeth and tried to get her head out of the clouds. Jillian understood they had tangled relations, mainly through Maura. But that would not ensure a longer relationship. In fact, it would mean this was just going to be a fling. If they kept it light, no one would get hurt.

And for the first time in a long time, she wanted more. She shook her head and tried to dismiss that idea.

When she was cleaned up and had gotten herself under some control, she grabbed a shirt out of her dresser, slipped it on, and then headed out to breakfast.

He spared her a glance as he slipped a waffle onto her plate. "Taking a little too long there, Jillian."

His voice was calm, but she heard the steel beneath it.

"I was trying to make sure my brain was working."

His lips twitched. "I have to say I'm pretty proud of myself."

She poured syrup on her waffles and shot him a look. "Why is that?

"You've got one of the sharpest minds I've ever encountered. If I screwed with it, then I am pretty sure I'm a god, like you said."

She chuckled, enjoying this whimsical side of him. She was pretty sure the only person in the world who had seen it, other than possibly his lovers, was his sister. Conner had never struck her as someone with a great sense of humor. The teasing was starting to get to her, though. He was all tough on the outside and somewhat gooey on the inside. That combination was deadly to her mind.

She was in serious trouble now.

"Eat. I didn't slave over these for you to just sit there and look at me."

She sighed and did that. "I had no idea that you could cook like this."

"I had to learn. Maura's kind of a picky eater."

She snorted. "Kind of? She makes Meg Ryan in *When Harry Met Sally* look like a pushover. I have never known anyone who went through a cafeteria line and made them cook stuff to order."

"She's always been like that. I remember when she was born, from the first she was pushing to get her way."

Jillian nodded. "She was a pill. I think that has a lot to do with genetics, but also the people who raised her, including you. Never once did I ever hear her say you doubted her or told her she shouldn't do something."

"I was glad when she started learning there were certain things that a brother did not want to hear."

She laughed at the pained look on his face. "I can imagine. How much of this does she know about?"

"This? You heard me talking to her."

"No, I mean this life of yours. You have to know she's dabbled in the lifestyle."

"Please, don't. I still think she's a virgin."

She shook her head at his joke and took another bite.

"What had you so upset yesterday?"

She glanced up, surprised. "Family. Just the family. They can be a pain in the ass, and dealing with them...there is a reason I'm not living on the mainland."

"Any reason in particular?"

"Same stuff. Money. It is the root of everything that is wrong in the Bentley family."

He didn't look happy, and she knew why. She wasn't being completely forthcoming.

"It isn't anything I want to rehash."

"Don't women like to talk about these kinds of things? Discuss feelings?"

"Not this. My family is a constant embarrassment to me. I'm just glad you took me out of the house and got my mind off them. It really helped me yesterday."

He smiled at that and looked down at her plate. "How do you not gain weight?"

She smiled. "When I'm deep in a book, I sometimes forget to eat most of the day. I guess when I'm not in the zone, I make up for it. It was delicious by the way."

She leaned forward and gave him an impulsive kiss that surprised both of them. When she sat back, he took her hand. "How far do you want to take this? Do you want to chalk up last night to some kind of insanity, or do you want to find out more about yourself?"

"About myself?"

Conner studied her fingers for a moment and then looked up at her. "The lifestyle is sometimes intense, and it teaches us things that we might not have known about ourselves."

"Like your need to dominate?"

He nodded. "And yours to submit. Sometimes it's just what you need to feel complete in the bedroom. But many times, it is more than that. It can reach into your soul. With me, I will expect that. I want all of you in that bedroom. Exploring this with you will probably be one of the greatest highlights of my life."

She noticed that he didn't profess love or tell her it was forever. She respected him for that, and while she might want to hear those words at some point, she wasn't sure she was ready for them.

He looked up at her with one eyebrow raised. "Indeed? Last night wasn't that intense."

She knew from experience and research it hadn't been, not for someone like him. For her, it had been a little mind-blowing. Jillian wouldn't tell him that.

He slipped his large hand between her legs and massaged her thigh. It was barely anything, but the touch had her body shimmering with heat. He kissed her, keeping his hand on her leg. She closed her eyes and enjoyed the way her body started to melt at the simplest of seductions.

Soon though, it wasn't enough for him, apparently. He picked her up off his lap. She expected him to take her to the bedroom, but instead he plopped her on the table.

He spread her legs as he leaned down and set his mouth on her pussy. Damn, the man had one of the most talented tongues. He should probably bronze the damn thing. He slipped inside, and she should have been embarrassed by how wet she was, but she didn't really care.

He replaced his mouth with his hand, sliding two fingers inside of her and pressing his thumb against her clit.

"Don't come, or there will be hell to pay."

She looked down at him as he watched her. Jillian wanted to close her eyes, to slip into the pleasure of his ministrations, but she couldn't. The way he was looking at her demanded his attention. She inched closer to her release and tried hard not to come, tried her best. As soon as she felt she couldn't hold back any longer, he stopped and pulled his hand away. He picked her up off the table and she thought he would take her to the bedroom then, but he didn't. He placed her on the rug a few feet away.

"Up on your knees and open that dirty mouth."

She could barely think. When she rose, it actually ached. She pressed her thighs together, trying to gain relief.

"Bad girl. Spread those legs so I can see your pussy. Again, you don't get relief unless I give it to you. You take and I will make sure you regret it."

There was a bit of a challenge in his voice, one that made her think he almost wanted her to do it, to come and then he could come up with some kind of nasty retribution. Instead, she did as he said.

"Ah, good."

He undid his shorts and let them fall to the floor so he could step out of them. She leaned forward, but he stopped her.

"Wait."

He pulled her shirt up and over her head, placing it on the chair behind him.

He left her there kneeling on the floor, waiting, but he soon returned with the blue scarf.

"Hands behind your back."

She did and almost fell over. He steadied her so she could find her balance before securing her hands behind her.

"Yeah, I like that." His voice shimmered with the arousal

that was now pulsing through her blood, pounding at her with every breath she took.

He walked in front of her and took his cock in his hand. He stroked himself as he watched her. "If I was in the mood, I could leave you like that, no relief while I took mine. But, you do have a talented mouth and I want it wrapped around my cock."

He walked up to her and rubbed the tip of it against her lips. His nostrils flared.

"Open up, baby."

Jillian usually didn't like endearments like that, but Conner had a way of saying it that made her want to please him. She opened her mouth not wanting to wait any longer. The first taste of him danced over her taste buds. Salty, sweet, and she craved it more than anything else right now. He moved in and out of her mouth since she couldn't due to her position. He slipped his fingers through her hair and plunged deep each time. She felt the head of his cock bump the back of her throat but she didn't care. With each thrust into her mouth, he pushed her closer to the edge. Her mind was concentrating on nothing but giving him satisfaction.

He pulled out of her mouth abruptly, and she almost fell forward. She would have if he hadn't been holding her. He cupped her and leaned down to give her a kiss. It was rough, wet, and she could feel it all the way to the soles of her feet. It caused her heart to beat completely out of control. By the time he pulled back, they were both breathing heavy. He leaned his forehead against hers, and when he brushed her braids back over her shoulder, she saw his hands were shaking.

At least he was affected by this as much as she was. He drew in a deep breath and then stepped back. He moved to the side and then helped her up.

"I think we should move this to the bedroom."

He guided her into her room, and she felt a shiver of anticipation. He hadn't done that much to her, and Jillian knew there was a part of her that wanted to obey and get rewarded. But there was that bad part of her, the one that wanted to push him into punishing her. It hadn't even been twenty-four hours since their first time together and she was already going out of her mind.

He stopped in front of the bed. "We don't have a lot to play with, unfortunately, but I plan on stopping by Rough 'n Ready later today."

She did have some things, but she wasn't sure if she should tell him. She had never used any of it, but she was a hands-on researcher. She didn't like describing something in her books if she didn't know the mechanics.

He must have read it in her face because he asked, "What?"

"I have a few toys."

She couldn't read his face then. It was as if all his emotion was hidden behind a mask.

"Really?"

She didn't know if he was granting her permission to speak or not.

"What do you have?"

"Riding crop, shibari ropes, and nipple clamps."

"Hmm," was all he said. It vibrated in his throat. "And you have used these?"

Oh, apparently he didn't like that idea, and she couldn't help but feel a little satisfied. The fact that he was a jealous shouldn't make her feel this good but it did.

"No."

That caught his attention. "No?"

"I bought it for research. They are in the bottom right drawer in my dresser."

He paced in front of her slowly, then stopped beside her. He untied her wrists. "Get them for me."

He sat down on the bed and waited. She walked to her dresser. Each step aggravated her already out-of-control arousal. Her labia was soaking wet, and she couldn't even imagine waiting much longer, but she knew he was going to make her. Conner didn't sound too happy that she hadn't told him about them. She retrieved them, feeling a little odd. She wasn't ashamed of her body. She had no problem being naked in front of others. This was different in some way.

She pulled out the crop and brought it over to him. He looked at her.

"Where are the other things?"

She shook her head. "The ropes are packed away, so I would have to find them. And the nipple clamps..."

His lips twitched. "Not your thing?"

She shook her head. "I like a little pain, but that is just beyond my acceptance."

"You might change your mind. If you do, let me know." He smiled and held out his hand. She gave him the crop. Conner studied it and slipped it through his fingers before smacking his opposite hand with it.

"Nice." His voice had deepened even more. "Hands on the bed and show me that pretty ass of yours."

She did as ordered, but now that a little of her arousal had been controlled, she did it slowly. Jillian really wanted to see how far she could push him.

"Do it now, Jillian, and do it fast."

She placed her hands on the foot of the bed and bent over.

He slipped the crop down her back, tracing her spine with it down to her ass, but instead of hitting her, he slipped it between her legs. She drew in a quick breath when he brushed it against her sex. It was the barest of touches—enough to tease but nothing else. She moved to get closer, but he chuckled and moved it away.

"Being naughty, Jillian?" he asked.

She wanted to be mad at the tone in his voice. It was the self-satisfied smirk she heard that usually had her temper rising, but this time she couldn't be mad. With that, there was a healthy dose of arousal threading his voice. Jillian knew he was under control to a point. Any man who could withstand a blowjob and not come like he did had immense control. There was something there that told her if she pushed him, they would both be rewarded by her punishment.

She moved again, and he sighed. It was part act, because it sounded like he was irritated, but she knew better. She knew that he wanted to punish her, wanted to smack her. And, dammit, she wanted him to do that.

He pulled the crop from between her legs and then smacked her ass. The sharp sound was loud in the silence of her house and arousing. The smack sent ripples of heat gliding over her flesh. He did it again, and she almost came. This was different than his hand. It was smaller and the pain a little sharper. He moved to her other cheek and smacked it hard. Again and again. Heat spread through her body, her pussy clenching with each smack. She could feel herself dampening as he smacked her. He stopped and pressed his palm against her hot skin.

"You are definitely made for spanking, Jillian."

She moaned when he continued to spread his hand over her

ass and smack her other cheek again. When he stopped, she felt as if her ass was on fire. He was breathing heavily.

"You will learn that you will not be able to move, to take your pleasure. If we had the time, I would give the punishment you deserve."

The idea had her brain spinning. She had a feeling that Conner could be very precise in his punishments, and dammit, she wanted that. What woman wouldn't?

"You aren't really ready for what I want to do to you."

She turned and looked over her shoulder at him. "What makes you say that?"

His eyes narrowed, and he smacked her ass again. The new pain slipped through her, and she closed her eyes and shivered.

"On the bed, face up."

He was abrupt. She was thrilled. Just challenging him was fun and apparently a turn-on for him. She did as ordered, ready for the next bit of fun. He set the crop on the side table.

Conner walked around the bed, his erection easy for her to see. He had no trouble with his nudity that was for sure. And with such a specimen, she was glad for it.

"One of the things new subs have issues with is understanding their place."

She could tell he wasn't happy with her by his tone.

"I thought you might be a little more open to it. Maybe understand that my control of your body during our love-making was the ultimate goal." He shook his head as if he were disappointed. "You have another lesson to learn."

He sat beside her on the bed. As he skimmed his hands over her body, she started to close her eyes.

"No. Look at me."

She couldn't seem to do it, to make herself look at him.

"Jillian, open your eyes right now or you will earn a punishment you might not want to deal with."

She willed herself to look at him.

"I keep saying this, but your pleasure is mine to give. You don't get to decide. In this we have to agree, or I will stop. Of course, a little lesson right now in my power over you should do."

She felt a lick of fear at the warning. Not that she thought he would hurt her, but she knew he was going to start pushing her boundaries, and Jillian wasn't so sure she was ready.

He slipped his hand down her body and skimmed his index finger along her slit.

"You will not come until I give you permission, do you understand me?"

She didn't answer right away, and he gave her clit piercing a tug.

"Do you?"

"Y-yes."

Lightly, he moved his fingers over her pussy. It was almost playful, but she knew his intent. With each barely-there touch, he heightened her need and pushed her further to the edge of her release. Her eyelids grew heavy, but he smacked her pussy.

"No. You will continue to look at me."

He dipped his fingers into her, and she sighed. The little move, along with pressing a finger against her clit, had her shivering. She was close, so close. Each time he moved his fingers, she grew damper and her inner muscles clamped a little harder around his fingers. Each thrust pushed her, and she felt herself tipping into her orgasm...he pulled his hand away.

"No, I didn't give you permission."

She pressed her thighs together, and he chuckled.

"Spread your legs. I don't want to have to warn you of that again."

She did, but she took her time. He looked back up at her, and when he noticed she continued to look at him, he smiled. "What a good girl."

He gave her pussy another little pat. The small movement had another heat rolling through her body.

"You don't want to experience what I would do to you if you don't learn this lesson."

She didn't say anything as he pinched her nipples.

"You have the perfect breasts." He bent down and took one into his mouth, grazing his teeth over the tip of it. Every time he did that, she felt it all the way to her cunt. He sat back up.

"See, if you can't learn this lesson, I will tie you to the bed and leave you like this for a while. Can you imagine lying here, aroused, that pussy so wet, ready to be fucked, but gaining no relief? I would do it."

There was no doubt in her mind that he would. She must have lost her mind because she found it somehow arousing.

"But, if you learn your lesson, we won't have to do that. I can imagine it, though. I would have your legs tied apart, that pussy in view for me while you laid here wanting to come so badly it hurt." He hummed, and she swore she felt the vibrations filter over her skin. "That might not be a bad thing."

He slipped his hand between her legs again, and she felt herself moving to her orgasm. In and out he moved his finger, adding another one as he tugged and pressed against her clit ring. He held her gaze, daring her to look away, but she didn't. Her breathing increased, and she was very aware of her breasts, of how hard her nipples were.

Soon, when she was very close to coming, he pulled his

hand away and picked up the condom. He put it on then covered her body with his. He leaned up on his elbows and looked down at her. Some kind of emotion came and went in his gaze before she could figure out what it was. Then, slowly, he leaned down and gave her a kiss. The sweetness had her heart turning over. It was a moment that came and went so fast she wasn't sure it happened, but in the next instant, he rose to his knees, lifted her hips off the bed and entered her in one hard thrust.

She was so aroused she almost came then. He must have felt it because he moved at a leisurely pace, not allowing her the release she needed.

Soon though, he was caught up in it and he said, "Come, Jillian, now."

For a moment, she couldn't. She had wanted it so fucking bad a minute ago. Now, she couldn't. He pressed against her clit and said, "Do it now."

She did in the next second. The orgasm hit her hard, causing her to bow off the bed and shake with the force of it. All the tension he had built up came surging forward in an explosion. As she started to come down from it, Conner sped up his thrusts so hard, the headboard was smacking against the wall. He pressed hard against her clit again and she came a second time before she had recovered from her first orgasm. This time he followed her, thrusting into her one last time and moaning her name.

Moments later, he collapsed, and she immediately slipped her arms around him. He kissed her cheek and rose up to look at her.

"Don't cry, Jillian."

She hadn't realized she was. "I..." She lifted her hand to brush away the wetness. "I didn't realize I was."

He kissed her, and she could tell he was satisfied. He nuzzled her neck again, and she felt a huff of breath as he apparently settled in for a while.

"Don't you have somewhere to go?"

He nodded and nipped at her jaw. She could tell the action was more one of comfort than sexual. She would have never guessed Conner was a snuggler.

"But I have some time, and I would rather get some rest. You wear an old man out."

She chuckled and kissed his forehead. "I guess I can live with that."

Jillian knew she was sunk right then and there. The man was a hard-ass Dom, definitely Alpha, but he would rather spend his morning snuggling with her. When he left it was going to hurt, more than she could probably imagine.

But, she couldn't stop herself now. She knew from her experience with her parents that she couldn't live life by waiting. You had to grab hold of happiness no matter how long it could last. As she drifted off to sleep, she realized that was exactly what she would do with Conner...and to hell with the consequences.

ten

Conner stepped into the Wailana Coffee House and was immediately hit with the smells he associated with a good diner, although there was a hint of Asian flavor to it. He noticed a mixture of people, some definitely locals and some tourists, as he looked around for Maria Callahan. He found her sitting in the back corner booth by herself. He hadn't been too sure that the steely-eyed fiancé would let her meet with him alone. She had her laptop open, and she was tapping away on the keys. He watched her for a moment, trying to mesh the woman she was when he trained her and the woman she was now. She looked...better, even happy. In all the years he had known her, he couldn't remember her ever looking that way. Satisfied? Yeah, he had seen that, but there was a softness about her that told him she was finally, truly content.

He had known from the start that she wasn't going to fit in with the bureau. Or he should say, she wouldn't have been happy there for long. She would succeed; her father had never given her that choice. Big John wouldn't have allowed for anything else. Conner might have made some choices based on

134

what was right for him and Maura, but she still had choices. He knew that John had never given Maria those.

She sat back and looked around. He knew the moment she saw him because she smiled, then waved. He walked down the aisle as she rose out of the booth and easily gave him a kiss on his cheek.

"You look good," he said, and he meant it.

He waited for her to sit, and he sat opposite of her. She smiled at him, and he couldn't help returning it. There was something so joyful about her that seemed to spill over to everyone in her vicinity.

"Thank you. My new career agrees with me." She patted the laptop next to her on the table.

He shook his head. "I would have never thought you would walk away from the FBI. In fact, I thought you were still there."

She cocked her head to the side and frowned at him. "I thought you would have known about it before now."

He nodded. "I've been working too many hours lately to keep up with friends."

She opened her mouth to say something, but the waiter interrupted her response. Still, he knew better than to think that he was off the hook. They both ordered, and she surprised him by ordering a side of spam with her eggs for lunch.

"Eating like a local?" he asked when the waiter left them alone.

She laughed. "I *am* a local. We decided to stay here since we both love it, and Rome has a good job."

"He works with Honolulu PD?"

She nodded and smiled. "I talked to your sister. She said you were supposed to be here relaxing. I hope you are doing that."

"You called my sister? You know my sister?" he asked.

She rolled her eyes. "Remember that weekend she came to see you? We've kept in touch on and off."

He frowned. "Why would she do that?"

"I don't know, maybe because she needed a woman near her age to talk to?" Sarcasm dripped from her voice.

"She could talk to me," he grumbled.

"Oh, that would have gone over well." She chuckled. "I understand you met one of her dates at the door wearing your shoulder holster."

He could feel heat creeping into his cheeks. "I'd just gotten home from work. And don't tell me if you have daughters, that cop of yours won't do the same thing."

She rolled her eyes. "He probably will, but I have a few years to worry about that." She shrugged. "Anyway, she just needed a sounding board, and I was happy to be it every now and then. It was better than dealing with, well, you know."

Her life. From an early age she had accompanied her father on the job. Conner was sure that she didn't have many dates in high school, and not because her father didn't allow it. John had been a shit father, that was for sure. No, it was because she was so focused on learning everything she could from him.

"Also, I've been chatting with her online for research. I'm writing a romantic suspense."

"You need my sister for that? You're ex-FBI."

"I needed to get an answer about some procedures in Florida law that you have to deal with. Plus, I needed to know what it was like on the Miami scene. My book takes place there."

"You could have asked me," he said as the waiter showed up with their drinks.

"You don't answer your emails."

He made a face, but he couldn't argue with her on that. He had been bad about answering emails and keeping up with friends all around. Unless it had to do with the job for the last year, he hadn't made much time for anything else.

She sipped her coffee then looked at him over the rim of the cup with an expression that reminded Conner of her father. Maria might not be made for the FBI, but she wasn't a shrinking daisy.

"And don't think you got me off track. She said you had chest pains. Please take that seriously."

"I'm here, aren't I?"

She shook her head. "Somewhat, but not really. The only reason you don't have updates from the office is because your sister won't let you have them."

"She called me this morning about work, so maybe you should be talking to her about not stressing me out."

"If she did, there is a good chance she had no other choice. She controls Zeke better than she does you."

"I don't know why he does that. Boy should know better than to let a woman boss him around.

"I'm sure it has something to do with the fact that he's in love with her."

That gave him pause. "What makes you say that?"

"He's a big tough man, and he's doing what she wants. He's your friend, but he does what she wants." She shrugged. "He's in love."

He pushed that aside. It was bad enough he knew they had some kind of sexual thing going. Conner really wasn't sure what it was, but he knew that their trip to Hawaii the year before had been the precipice for it. It had only gotten worse since they'd returned. Love was another matter, one that he didn't even want to contemplate himself, let alone his best friend and only sibling.

"So, you're getting married?" he asked.

Her smile widened, and she looked so young. He knew she was about the same age as Jillian, but he had always thought of Maria as older. Now, though, she looked younger than his sister. In all the time he'd known her, he had never seen her smile like that, and it did his heart good to see it.

"Isn't he cute? I just couldn't keep my hands off him."

He shook his head. "How did you meet?"

"The Dom case. I put myself undercover."

"Of course you did."

"He liked women who looked like me." She shrugged as if it were no big deal. "It worked."

And in her mind, that was what was important. It was one of the reasons he'd walked away from the FBI. Anything to win the case wasn't his way anymore. He was relentless, but he definitely wasn't a man who would think putting himself into a trap was a good idea. Not when he'd had his sister to take care of at the time.

"And so you met with Carino when you came here to work?"

She smiled at him. "Yes. He wasn't too happy about having to play with the FBI, but then he started to like it. A lot."

The conversation was starting to transform into something he knew would embarrass him. She might have been his trainee, but Maria had been almost like a younger sister to him.

"Do you know what you're doing with him?"

"He's marrying me, isn't he?" She laughed. "Oh, my God, your expression. Yes, I do know what I'm doing with him."

He let one eyebrow rise as the waiter set the plates in front of them.

She laughed. "I do. He lets me be myself, and I like that. He was the first person in my life who didn't really look at me as Callahan's daughter."

"I didn't see you that way."

She shook the salt over her scrambled eggs. "No, you saw me as a little sister, and I saw you as a big brother as soon as I got over my crush."

"Crush?" he asked.

"Yeah, when I was about sixteen, I had a major crush on you."

He felt his face heating, and she laughed. "I got over it when you told me I wasn't that smart. I was a little crushed, but then I proved you wrong."

He remembered the case then. Maria had been convinced the killer was a woman, and they all told her she was crazy. She had been proven right.

"You have to come to the wedding," she said, breaking into his thoughts.

"I didn't get an invitation."

She frowned. "I sent you one a month ago."

Shit. He probably did get one, but he missed it thanks to his work. "Well, then I'm coming."

"I'm registered at Macy's."

"Who said I'm buying you anything?"

"I did, and it better be nice or I'll tell Maura. It's this Saturday at the Hilton chapel. Dress is Hawaiian formal, which means anything can go," she said with a laugh.

"Yeah? Can I bring a date?"

"Sure, especially if it's Jillian Sawyer. I had no idea you knew her. I would love to pick her brain."

"Why?"

"You do realize she is considered one of the smartest authors out there, right? She always hits the *New York Times* and *USA Today*. She had a huge contract with NY publishers and walked away from it. She was one of the first authors to sell a million downloads. I would love to talk to her about it."

And it was then that he realized he didn't know. He never asked her about her work. It was a habit of his because there was so much of his job that he couldn't talk about, so he tended to not discuss it at all. But now he realized that he should have.

"Well it is, and I'm sure she wouldn't mind. Since you both live here, it would probably be easy for you to hook up. How about next week?"

She laughed. "You haven't changed."

"What?"

Maria shook her head and swallowed a sip of coffee. "Conner, I'll be on my honeymoon."

He chuckled. "Yeah, I guess you would be on a honeymoon. Where does someone who lives in Hawaii go for a honeymoon?"

"Tahiti. I have always wanted to see it, so Rome made it happen."

From the looks the cop had been giving her the other night, Conner was pretty sure if she asked for a trip to Venus, Carino would probably figure out a way to do it.

"I don't have to ask you if he makes you happy, because he apparently does."

"He makes me feel whole. That's all that matters."

And that is when it hit him. When he had been in bed with

Jillian that morning, he had felt something squeeze his heart. Instead of comfort, it had felt like something had grabbed him by the balls. He was desperately falling for Jillian. There was a part of him he held back from everyone, but not Jillian. She might have to tug it out of him, but he could be himself with her. He just didn't know what the fuck to do about it. Laying it on the line would leave him vulnerable, and he wasn't about to do that.

"Conner?"

He shook his head and noticed that Maria was staring at him with concern. "What?"

"Are you okay? You look a little odd there."

He shook off the feeling and smiled at her. "Yeah. Just realized something, but I will work it out."

She opened her mouth, but he held up his hand. "No, really, I'm fine. Tell me about your book."

And, he did his best to concentrate on her and not his worries about Jillian. Although, he had a feeling that no matter what, Jillian would always be there in his mind. And that scared him more than anything he'd faced in his life.

Jillian returned from her run on the beach a little more exhausted than usual. It had been a few days since she'd ran, and truth was, she hadn't been pushing herself during the last few days of her last book. The edits had gotten to her, along with the worry of Conner coming to stay with her. Now that he had been there a week, she knew she had been bad about getting out. Plus, add the sex to the equation and she was a little more worn out than she had expected.

As she approached her front door, she saw a package sitting on her doorstep. She frowned at it and then looked around the area. She saw Mick working on his bike.

"Hey, Mick have you seen anyone around here?"

He looked up from his bike. "No, love, sorry. I was out on the bike."

It was just a plain manila envelope with her name scrawled across the front of it. Gingerly, she picked it up between two fingers and shook it. It didn't sound like there was a lethal toxin in it, she thought with grim humor. She opened her front door and kicked it shut behind her. She walked over to her kitchen and opened the envelope. Glossy pictures spilled out onto the table. Her heart stuttered to a stop.

They were pictures of her. On the beach, on her lanai, with Conner. Jesus, there was even one with her in her bra and panties. The front door opened and she whirled around, a scream lodging in her throat when she saw Conner. He was smiling until he saw her face. The happy look dissolved.

"What's wrong?" he asked and rushed to her.

She handed him the pictures. She watched his face harden even more, his eyes steel when he looked at her.

"Where did you get this?" he asked. His voice had gone cold. A chill ran down her spine, and she had to cross her arms to try to warm herself.

"It was sitting on the front step when I came back from a run."

He carefully set the pictures down on the table and pulled out his phone.

"You're the only one who touched it?"

She nodded.

"Did you see anyone, anyone at all?"

She shook her head. "Mick was here when I got home, but he'd been out on a ride." Plopping down onto a chair, she shivered. "It's creepy."

"It's criminal is what it is." He was already dialing a number before she could stop him. She didn't want to, but there was a little part of her that worried. It would cause a ruckus, and she definitely didn't want it getting out to the public. She didn't want anyone to see the sickness in the pictures.

He apparently read her expression. "Don't even think about shrugging this off. Your name is on the front, and it wasn't mailed. Someone knows you live here."

She hesitated the barest of seconds then nodded. It was stupid not to have it checked out. Still, maybe they could keep it under wraps and she could keep her location secret. She enjoyed being another transplanted mainlander.

"Hey, Maria, I was wondering if Rome was around. We have a situation here with Jillian."

He was quiet for a second. "Rome, yes, it seems that Jillian might have a stalker. Sure." He rattled off the address.

He hung up and looked at her. "Thanks for not fighting me on this. I have a feeling we would lock horns, and while I would win, you wouldn't be that happy with me."

She rubbed her arms again. She had been so hot just minutes before, and now she couldn't seem to get warm. "That would be stupid. I'm just not that happy about having a cop in my house. They tend to stick their noses into things."

He gave her a grin that damn near stopped her heart. "What about me?"

She stared at him for a second then said, "You don't count. You're not FBI anymore, and well, you are kind of good in bed.

So, I can forget about the cop thing. Unless you have some handcuffs we can use."

"Later," he promised as he reached for her and pulled her into his arms. His body heat warmed her, and she started to shiver. The enormity of the situation hit her then. It seemed like such a simple thing, a plain envelope. But it had changed everything. Now she thought about everything she had done the last few days and wondered how much of it the creep had watched.

"Are you okay?" he asked, his voice vibrating against her ear.

She nodded and snuggled closer, taking the comfort he offered. The raw scent of him tickled her senses and somehow calmed her. She sighed. "I hate to say it, but I kind of missed you today."

He brushed his mouth against her temple. "I missed you, too. Did you keep yourself busy?"

"Wrote a few thousand on the new project. Then needed a run. I've been bad about that lately."

"You run?" he asked with enough surprise that she looked up at him.

"Yes. Do I look like I am out of shape?"

"No, it's just that running just doesn't seem to fit. I just thought you were naturally this shape."

She rolled her eyes. "Yeah, what does that mean?"

He sighed. "You're so 'go with the flow.' Living in the moment."

"Most of the time. But, with my career, I can't be too lazy. I find running keeps my mind focused. And I do spend most of my day in the chair. At the rate I eat, that could lead to disaster."

"Yeah, your career..."

She looked at him, but there was a knock at the door. She walked over and had her hand on the knob, but Conner stopped her. He gave her a look that told her it was stupid to even think of opening it.

"Who is it?" Conner asked.

"Mick and Adam."

He sighed with a hint of irritation and opened the door.

"We just wanted to check on Jillian."

Conner was blocking her from stepping in front of him. She could feel the testosterone rising in the room. "Why would you do that?"

"Because of the envelope," Adam said.

"What do you know about it?" Conner asked, and she heard the accusation in his voice.

With a groan she smacked him on the ass. He glanced over his shoulder at her with a look that told her she was pushing it a little too far.

Jillian rolled her eyes. "I asked him about it. He was working on his bike in the yard. God."

She pushed Conner aside. "Conner's already called the police."

She could tell that Mick wanted to ask more, but he glanced toward Conner and decided against it.

"Well, if you need anything, you have our numbers. We asked Jamie if she saw anything, and she didn't."

"Thanks, guys."

They were walking down the steps when a dark sedan pulled off Kam Highway and into her driveway.

"I guess that's your friend and her cop. That was quick."

"They live in Laie and were on their way home. They weren't very far away when I called." He watched them get out of the car. "Oh, and two warnings. Maria wants to ask you about writing, and we're going to their wedding this Saturday."

With that, he walked down the steps to greet his friends. The grim expression on his face was mirrored by the cop. He didn't look very happy. She didn't know if it was the situation or the fact that he had been on his way home. It was then that she realized Conner hadn't asked her to go to the wedding, he'd ordered her.

She didn't mind taking orders in the bedroom. If she had any doubts, last night and this morning had taken care of that. In fact, thinking about what he might do next time they were in bed had her body humming with need. Still, it didn't mean that she was going to accept him telling her what to do outside of the bedroom.

They would have to talk about it later because that wasn't really important right now. She followed him down the stairs and went to talk to the detective and his fiancée.

But they would talk about it. She might be a submissive when sex was involved, but the man needed to learn that she ran her life and no one else.

eleven

Conner watched as Rome looked over the letter. He might not be who he expected Maria to end up with, but Conner was damn happy he was on the HPD. Anyone with that determined look in his eye would definitely be of some use in this. He'd pulled a pair of gloves out of a box in his car and slipped them on before touching the pictures. Maria had brought in a plastic bag that Rome was now slipping the pictures into.

"I can have the lab take prints off it, but my guess is that the bastard didn't leave any." He looked up at Jillian. "Have you had issues with stalkers before?"

She shook her head.

"Are you sure?" Conner asked.

She rolled her eyes. "I think I would know if I had a stalker."

"No, not always," he said.

Her eyes narrowed, and she opened her mouth, but Maria stopped her.

"There's always a chance that you've had one and had no idea. Many times the first indication people get is an attack."

She shrugged. "It would be hard to track me. I doubt very

much this is someone interested in me because of my books. I know that people are never safe, not in today's world, but I've taken measures to make it harder for anyone to find me."

"What do you mean by that?" Maria asked.

"All of my mail goes to a post office box in Atlanta. My PA picks it up and handles it."

"Does she send it to you?" Rome asked.

Jillian glanced at him. "No. She scans it and emails it to me. I really don't get that much physical mail since people use email more often."

"And she's the contact on your website?" Maria asked.

Jillian nodded.

"Then we need to know what she doesn't forward to you. There might be some of it she just deletes."

"Anyone could track you through her," Conner said.

"I don't know how. I have a direct deposit that goes into her account monthly. I am an LLC that is based in Georgia, so all my banking is done there. No one knows where I live."

"Even your family?" he asked.

She made a face. "Especially my family. They know I live on an island somewhere, but they have no idea where. I have an idea they think it's somewhere in the Caribbean. Plus, I have a Georgia cell phone number."

"If the stalker had access to phone records, he could figure it out," Maria said. "Any kind of cell phone tower hit would definitely give him the location you were in last."

"Whoa, I don't have a stalker. Probably. Okay, it isn't a sure thing, but let's not go crazy about this. I agree that it needs to be checked out."

"There are many ways to find a person, especially today," Maria said. "You are very visible online."

"Who knows where you live?" Conner asked.

"You, your sister, and knowing your sister and her relationship with him, Zeke. Then there are a handful of writers who I've met up with here. But for the most part, I keep it pretty secret. I don't want anyone to know where I live."

"So you were worried about a stalker already?"

She shook her head. "My family. With my grandmother's will, they are stuck getting my approval on everything. I wouldn't put it past one of those lazy bastards to show up here on a regular basis to try to get my approval for all kinds of crap. So I keep it secret from everyone except Charles."

"Charles?" he asked a little too sharply. That earned him an annoyed look from Jillian and a knowing smile from Maria.

"He's the lawyer in charge of the family money. Because of the terms of the will, he needs to know where I am at all times."

He nodded, but he was going to ask her more about her personal life. Granted, he doubted that it was an ex. He had a feeling that Jillian kept her privacy. Still, you never know how many people you touch in a given day. Hell, it could be someone at the swap meet that she saw on a regular basis. Including the asses who had the house beside her.

"I'm going to take this back to the lab right now. Trail of evidence," Rome said. He glanced at Conner. "Wanna come with me?"

He didn't want to. He wanted to stay and ask Jillian about her ex lovers. And everyone else she talked to. There was something she was hiding from him, and he didn't like it. But he probably needed to talk to Rome privately, and he needed time to cool down.

"I can stay here with Jillian," Maria offered.

He didn't know if she did that because she saw the look in

his eyes or if she wanted to ask Jillian work questions. It was probably a little of both. And, she might find out more from Jillian than he could. The idea that he was so jealous of her exes wasn't a good sign.

"Okay. Call if anything else happens."

Jillian rolled her eyes as Maria and Rome walked outside to give them some privacy.

She settled her hands on her hips and looked at him. "I think I can handle myself, Dillon."

He stepped up to her, grabbed her by the arms, yanked her forward and kissed her. When he pulled back, he touched her forehead to his. "Just promise me you will listen to Maria."

She pulled back and looked into his eyes. "Okay."

He studied her, trying to figure out if she was lying or not.

"I promise. I'm not stupid, Conner. I know that this is serious. I will not hide because of it, but I won't take any stupid chances. Plus, I'll listen to the woman who used to be an FBI agent. I am not an idiot."

"I didn't say you were. I just want you to understand that you need to be careful."

He could tell he had offended her, but he didn't care. He would rather have her safe and pissed off than hurt. Still, she didn't seem to hold it against him. She leaned forward and gave him a sweet, soft kiss that had him groaning. Within seconds it turned hot. He pulled back and rested his forehead against hers again.

"This guy is pissing me off. I had some toys to play with tonight."

She smiled. "Well, then, you better hurry back here, stud."

Maria cleared her throat discreetly from behind him.

He sighed. "Behave."

She nodded and watched him leave, saying nothing else. He trotted down the steps to the sedan where Rome waited for him.

"How long have you known Jillian?" Rome asked as he pulled out onto Kam Highway.

"About ten years."

Rome glanced at him.

"No, not like that. She was my sister's roommate in college. I knew her, but not really. When I was ordered to take a month off, my sister decided to get me as far away from the office as possible. She called Jillian and rented the room from her for me. Not to mention that she bought the ticket."

The detective glanced at him from the corner of his eye. His lips twitched. "It's killing you, isn't it?"

He snorted. "Like the devil. Of course, Jillian helps me take the edge off."

"I had a feeling about that. Micah vouches for her, so I have a feeling she's a good egg. And Maria is positively giddy about talking to her."

"She's changed a lot since the last time I saw her."

"Maria?"

"Yeah. I have to say you are probably the reason."

He pulled to a stop at a light and glanced over at Conner. "So, you've known Maria for a long time?"

"Yeah," Conner said, more comfortable with this line of questioning. "I knew her when she was just a teenager. Even then she was a know-it-all pain in the ass."

Instead of getting mad, Rome's lips twitched. Apparently the man knew exactly who he was marrying. Maria was a good person, but she was often times too sure she was right about things. Worse, she usually was right and never let you hear the end of it.

"Was her father as much of a bastard as I think he was?" Rome asked.

Conner nodded. "He was my mentor, and without him I probably wouldn't have made it in the FBI. But he was a shitty father."

"You were in sort of the same situation from what Maria said with your sister."

Conner shook his head as Rome pulled out onto H-3. "No. Maura was a little older than Maria was when her mother died. She'd already been accepted to University of Georgia and was entering a year early by the time our folks were killed in a car crash. Plus, I was lucky she got paired up with Jillian the first year. She sort of took Maura under her wing."

"But, if she hadn't been that old or going off to college? If you had been forced to make the decision...."

He glanced over at Rome and realized that he was weighing and measuring Conner on some level.

"I would have walked away without a thought because family is more important than anything in the world."

Rome shot him a smile. "That's the way it is in my family. Maria's was a little screwy. I'm just hoping I can get her over the fear that she doesn't know how to be a parent. She about faints every time I mention that I want to have at least three kids. Being the Italian Catholic I am, I really want more, but I don't mention that."

"Good luck with that one."

Rome nodded. "Going to need it, but not any more than you are going to need, right? I mean, are you planning on settling here in the islands?"

It wasn't until that moment that the idea slipped into his mind. He didn't need to live in Miami to run the company. He could stay here, be with Jillian...and slowly go crazy. He wasn't made for Hawaii any more than she was made for some place like DC or Miami. Jillian belonged here and he didn't.

"No. My business is in Miami, so I'm only here for the month."

If Conner didn't sound that convincing, Rome said nothing about it. Conner was pretty sure the detective didn't believe him, but it was the way it would have to be. They both had obligations and lifestyles.

It was just the way it was.

Jillian had been trying to keep the conversation going with Maria, but it kept trailing off. Jillian was pretty sure she knew what was going on.

"Go ahead."

"What?"

"I don't mind you asking about the business. It will probably take my mind off things right now. Let's get comfortable in the living room."

Maria practically skipped into the room. If her nerves weren't shot, Jillian would get a kick out of her. Newbies could sometimes irritate Jillian, but there nothing like being around a novice still excited about the business. Once they settled down, Maria didn't hesitate to start her questioning. After ten minutes, Jillian did not have a doubt that the woman had been an excellent FBI agent. She shot questions at her as if Jillian was a suspect.

A flash of light brightened the room telling Jillian the guys were finally home.

"I didn't think they would ever get home."

Maria smiled. "One thing you should be used to here on the island is the leisurely pace."

"I guess. I'm just a little on edge."

"Of course, you are. Hell, I know I would be."

She studied the former agent. "I don't think anything would bother you."

Maria waved that away. "I'm just really good at hiding it. Like talking to you about writing. I will probably pass out from the stress of it when I get home."

Jillian chuckled. "I would have never guessed."

"Well, I was very nervous. And excited. I haven't decided what to do, but I like that you are so open about the business part of it. I don't have to worry about money, thanks to my father's royalties, but it is nice to know there are more options out there these days."

Jillian hadn't even thought about John Callahan's work, but he had penned a few *New York Times* best sellers on the nonfiction list. And many of them stayed up there even today.

The door opened, and Conner came in with a grim look on his face.

"Nothing yet, before you ask. It will take a few hours to get into the lineup to be tested. I doubt they will find much, but it's worth a try."

Rome followed him in. "There was a double homicide in Waikiki, so you know that's going to take precedence."

She nodded. "Makes sense. Did you want something to drink before you head home?"

He shook his head. "Just need my bed...not to mention my woman. I hope she didn't make you feel like a bug on a lens."

Maria shot him a look that told him he would be in trouble for that later on. "No one else thinks that. Just you." She turned her attention back to Jillian. "Thanks again for all your help. I'll send those chapters to you tomorrow. And you," she said as she gave Conner a kiss on the cheek, "don't forget about my gift. I expect something nice."

"That's rude," Conner said, but Jillian could tell from his voice that he wasn't mad. In fact, his tone was very close to the way he talked to Maura.

"Nice doesn't work with you. And I know you can afford it."

With that, Rome tugged her out of the house, and Conner shut the door behind them.

"What took you so long to get back?" she asked

"I had Rome check out a few people for me."

"What people would that be?"

"Adam and Mick."

She shook her head. "There's no reason to check on them."

"Mick spends a lot of time paying attention to you."

"Yeah, well, he spends more time paying attention to Adam."

That had him stopping. "Oh?"

"I guess your snooping didn't tell you that, huh? Well, they've been living together for five years."

"They are both former Special Forces."

"Yeah, I know."

He frowned. "And you didn't tell me?"

"You didn't ask."

He settled his hands on his hips, his expression fierce.

"Dammit, Jillian, I'm not trying to be an asshole. I'm trying to find out who scared the hell out of you."

She took a breath. "I know that, but I know those guys."

"Well, I had a talk with them."

She felt the weight of his actions. She didn't like being watched over so much. Not really. "Shit. You have to know they would never hurt me."

"I do. After talking with them, they wanted to beat the living hell out of whoever scared you. Plus, they gave alibis for earlier today, and Jamie verified it." He paused and looked at her. "Are you sure they're together? There is something definitely going on with them and Jamie."

"Really? Well, I guess they could be bi, but even so, they are definitely together."

"How could you know? They don't act like it."

She chuckled. "What does that mean?"

"I live near South Beach, so I know a lot of bisexuals and gay men. Hell, my business partner is bi, and it doesn't bother me. They just don't act like a couple."

"Well, since I accidentally walked in on them having sex, I'm pretty sure they are."

He chuckled. "I guess that would prove it."

"Are you hungry?"

He smiled. "Yeah, a little."

"I've got the makings for pizza."

"Yeah? I heard from Maura it is the best around."

"Prepare to be wowed." She leaned up and gave him a kiss that had her body and her mind humming by the time she pulled away.

"Come on, you can help."

And the big bad Dom smiled, took her hand, and let her lead him into the kitchen.

———

"You're worried about this guy?" Micah asked him.

"Yeah. It's weird, but she's right. Jillian has made it virtually impossible to find her. Seriously. I never knew anyone worried about his or her privacy this much, and I handle private security. So the fact that someone has found her, and has had the ability to rattle her, is more than a little disturbing."

Micah studied him for a moment. The stoic Native American definitely could make anyone squirm.

"What?" he asked.

"You sure you're not blowing it out of proportion?"

Conner shook his head. He might be a little over the top but he knew better. His gut was telling him this was not something to ignore. "You didn't see the pictures."

"Okay, that is creepy as shit. There were some of them of you two alone?"

He nodded. "I have another worry I didn't tell her."

Another silent study from Micah. "That you think this has more to do with you than her?"

Conner should have known he would pick up on it. Micah had been a bounty hunter before he opened the premier BDSM club of the islands. When Dee ran away from Hawaii, it took Micah less than twenty-four hours to find her. His instincts would have made him a superb FBI agent, but Micah would have never fit in at the bureau. And there was that juvie record.

"Yeah. I don't know of anyone who would have a hard-on

for me this long other than Dee's family. They're still pissed at me."

"I'm sure they are. Having any problems with them?"

"No. Since several of them gave testimony, they are in hiding, so I doubt they would have the time or the money to do it. But, I did piss quite a few people off."

"You're going to have to go back through your cases."

He grimaced, thinking about it. "And, I either need the FBI to help—"

"Which will take forever."

Conner nodded. "Yes, or I need to get outside help."

"Use your resources."

"I can't. I do and Jillian will know."

"Talk to that business partner of yours."

He shoved his hand through his hair in frustration. "Who will do anything Maura tells him because unfortunately, as Maria pointed out, he is trying to get my sister back into bed."

Micah sighed and crossed his arms over his chest. "Damn, you're going to make me talk to my brother-in-law."

"If you could?"

"He's actually here for the wedding and in a shit mood. Maybe this will help. The only time he's nice is when he's around Dee"

"Why is he in a bad mood?"

Micah shrugged. "I've learned with that family you don't ask about bad moods unless you're in the mood for a fight, and there's a good chance something is going to get broken." He sighed theatrically. "Those Italians have world-class tempers on them."

Conner laughed. Dee and Devon's father had been organized crime, and both of them had gone into hiding when he'd put a hit out on them.

"I guess so," Conner said.

"I think it's more of one of those freaky-genius things. Devon has a through-the-roof IQ. He can't just sit around and not do anything. He's trying for Dee's benefit because they are attempting to rebuild their relationship, but you can feel him fighting it. Sitting in one spot just isn't good for him. So, if I give him something illegal to do, he might be in a better mood. Which in turn will make Dee happy."

"Which is a benefit to you."

He smiled. "But of course."

He shook his head. "What does she see in you?"

"I'm the man of her dreams."

As soon as he said it, the phone rang. Micah looked at the number and his expression softened. Conner didn't have to be told that it was Dee on the other end.

"Hey, babe. I was just talking to your FBI man."

He listened for a while and glanced at Conner. "Yeah, I guess he might be taken now. He has a job for Dev, so you can be free of him."

Another pause. "I have no idea if it's illegal, but I don't think we need to worry about it. Conner will take care of him."

Conner rolled his eyes. Like that family worried about legal. Granted both of them were somewhat legal now, although Devon still hid behind a fake name and persona. Conner didn't want to know the reasons. It was a constant reminder that he was on the run from something or someone, and Conner didn't want to get involved. One thing he knew, Devon could handle himself.

After Micah hung up, he looked at Conner. "Let's go."

"Where?"

Micah rose and started to shut off lights.

"My house. Devon has his own equipment and doesn't want to chance getting me in trouble here. Lord only knows what he does with those laptops he brings."

"Laptops. As in more than one?"

"Yeah. He has his own plane so he doesn't have to worry about any security."

He hesitated, and Micah smiled at him over his shoulder. "You might want to stop being worried about the legality of it. When someone you care about is in trouble, you throw all the rules out the window."

Conner nodded and followed him out of the office. He knew right now he would do anything to keep Jillian safe. And if it was someone from his past, Conner would make sure that none of the ugliness from his FBI past ever touched her.

twelve

Conner accepted the beer from Micah as he watched Devon's fingers play over the keyboard. The sharp-eyed man missed nothing, and that was probably the reason he had been recruited into the CIA at such an early age. He glanced at Micah then faced Conner.

"I can do it. It will actually be easy for me to handle. FBI isn't that hard to hack. First question though, don't you have all your cases?"

Conner nodded. "It's on the drive I gave you."

Devon glanced at Micah again, then back to him. "Why don't you just look it up?"

"What I have in there is just the cases. I don't know what happened to them after I left. Hell, convicts have been known to work out deals years later when they get sick of prison. So if the government made a deal, I wouldn't know. A lot of times they are listed on the official records as dead."

"It's been years since you were an agent," Micah pointed out.

"Like I said, it doesn't matter. They think they can get good testimony off someone, they will give them a deal. One guy was in for ten years and got a deal."

"Which you don't like?" Micah asked.

Conner shrugged. "It's a necessary evil that I understand. Unfortunately, many criminals know and will use what little they know to work one out. Many times the feds get fucked over. And I always loved working my ass off to get someone in prison only to have them back on the streets."

"What kind of meeting is going on in my house without my knowledge?" Dee asked as she walked into the living room.

Conner watched Micah's fierce expression soften as he rose to walk to his wife. It wasn't hard to see the Native American Dom was still madly in love with her after over a year of marriage.

"Your husband and his friend are trying to convince me to break the law."

She laughed. "Devon, really, I know you better than you know yourself. You would break the law faster than I can say luau."

She was glowing with the pregnancy. Just a few months along, she was barely showing. Of course, she was wearing some yoga pants and a shirt that looked to be Micah's, so it would be hard to tell. She had allowed her hair to go back to its natural dark color and had it in a ponytail on top of her head. If he didn't know her, he would expect she was a college coed and not a married woman approaching thirty and pregnant with her first child.

She gave her twin a kiss then did the same to Conner.

"So, what's going on?"

He glanced at Micah, who rolled his eyes. "If you don't tell her now, Devon will tell her. Those two tell each other everything."

"Not everything, thank God," Devon said with mock disgust dripping from his voice. "But if I didn't, you'd tell her, marshmallow."

Micah just smiled. "And happy to be one."

Dee settled her hands on her hips. "I ask once again, what the hell is going on?"

"Dillon wants me to make sure that no one he put in jail is out after a deal with the FBI."

She nodded as she took a seat on the couch. Micah sat next to her. "Why?"

"I'm afraid someone might be stalking Jillian." He gave her a rundown of the events of yesterday.

"Oh, that's horrible," Dee said. "What's Devon got to do with it?"

"I want to make sure it isn't from one of my old cases."

"All the pictures were taken after you arrived?"

He nodded, realizing no one else had picked up on that right away like Dee did.

"How sucky." She looked at her brother. "You're going to do it?"

He nodded. "It should take me a couple of hours."

"This is the FBI," Conner said, feeling defensive of his old profession.

"Yeah, so I might be giving them more credit than they should get."

And looking at the younger man's smirk, Conner realized he was probably right. The federal government was having a hard time staying on top of cyber crime. Every time they got a handle on something, hackers figured out another way to get in.

And now he was asking one of them to do just that.

"You have to let go of some of your hang-ups about the law, my friend," Micah said.

"I know. I understand that it has to be done this way, but I don't have to like it."

"You skirt the law all the time, Conner," Dee said with a smile. "At least this time it is for a really good reason."

He could tell by the look in her eye that Dee was making more out of his romance with Jillian than there should be. He didn't want to face the fact that every time the idea of someone stalking Jillian came up, he wanted to kill someone. It was natural due to his relationship with her.

And if he repeated that enough times, he might believe it himself.

"Want another beer?" Micah offered as he stood and took Conner's empty bottle.

"No thanks. Jillian should be done writing by now, so I'm going to head back."

"We'll see you tomorrow, right, at the wedding?" Dee asked.

"Sure."

They followed him out the door and stood there as they watched him drive away. Micah and Dee were a unit, together. His parents had been like that. They had a deep affection and friendship that Conner had always envied. He had never expected it for himself because he had seen too many relationships go bad. It had never bothered him before. Now, though, he wondered what he had missed out on.

He shook his head and turned onto H-3 to head back to

Jillian's. He couldn't think about those things, and he refused to regret his choices. Conner had made some mistakes, but he lived with them and moved on. Wanting more with Jillian was natural, but he couldn't get caught up in that. He didn't know if he had the heart for it.

thirteen

Jillian sank down below the bubbles and scented water. The sigh that escaped was definitely well earned. Eight straight hours at the computer. It had been long, but the story had flowed. With the craziness of the past few days, she hadn't had a really good chance to write like that. Well, since Conner had come to see her.

But that she couldn't regret. Since their first night together, she barely was able to contain herself. She wasn't a woman who got hearts and rainbows in her eyes over a man. She had learned at an early age that people let you down. With Conner, though, she couldn't seem to keep herself from doing that. In fact, more than once she would think back to the way he'd touched her the night before and her heart would sigh.

She closed her eyes and tried to blot it out. Hoping that she would have more to this relationship wasn't healthy. She needed to keep it light and easy, and then she wouldn't get hurt.

She heard his voice outside and knew he had returned. Within a couple of minutes, he was in the bathroom. "So, I go off to work and here you are being lazy in the tub."

She laughed and opened her eyes. And just like that, all those promises slid away. She didn't know what to do with a man that was this yummy, not to mention dependable. He had worn a pair of shorts again, and the tan that was now darkening his skin looked good on him. Healthy.

He was smiling at her, leaning against the doorjamb, and right there she gave up running. At that moment, she knew there would be no protecting herself.

"I worked hard today. Over eight thousand words, so suck it."

His eyebrows rose. "Eight thousand?"

She shrugged. "I tend to get in a zone and just go with it. It's a mess and needs to be edited, but I do better if it's all on paper rather than editing as I go."

He nodded as his gaze traveled down her body in the tub. It was one of the things she had put in since she moved in. Everything was utilitarian in the house except the tub. It was an over-sized claw foot, and it was her escape from work at times. He walked forward, his gaze on her face. What she saw there had her mind going blank. His eyes were dark, heated, and filled with a need she knew so well that it scared her. She felt a corresponding hunger flare to life within her. He reached the tub and looked down at her.

"I come home and find you lying here, smelling of a garden and looking beyond decadent. It's enough to make a man crazy."

There was enough of a lip on the tub for him to balance himself on the edge.

"So I take it you're done for the day?"

There was an edge to his voice that told her of the hunger building in him. Heat flared low in her tummy and all the moisture dried up in her mouth. He slipped his fingers over her nipple as it peeked up through the bubbles. They tightened instantly. After placing a hand on the other side of the tub, he balanced himself and lowered his head to take her nipple in his mouth. She closed her eyes and groaned. She had never been uncomfortable with her sexuality, but there was something slightly embarrassing that this man did this to her so easily. He had barely touched her, and she was ready to come.

He lifted his head and stood. "Out."

For a second, she didn't respond. Her damn mind was still trying to deal with the delicious heat rolling through her system. Apparently, he took it as disobedience.

"Out *now*."

This time, he was a bit more forceful in his direction. She stood as he'd ordered and stepped out of the tub. He held out his hand and helped. She was standing on the rug dripping wet, bubbles sliding down her body. He grabbed a towel and dried her. She wasn't expecting him to take so long, but she should have. It showed her who was in control, and while she had heard the arousal in his voice, she was sure it was there to prove to her that he could still control himself.

If she didn't like it, she would complain, but the truth of the matter was she loved it. There was something to be said for a man who could control himself. And it enticed her. What would it take to make him lose control?

He slid the towel over her body, paying special attention to her breasts, then slipped it down between her legs. He pressed against her pussy with his towel-draped fingers. She closed her eyes and released a steady breath.

"Same rules as before, Jillian. No coming without my command."

He pressed hard, and her knees buckled. The roughness of the cloth was creating such delicious friction that she felt herself dampen.

He dropped the towel and moved in behind her. "Hands on the counter."

She did as ordered.

"Spread those legs, Jillian. I want to see how wet that pretty little cunt of yours is."

Heat lanced through her at the words. She knew her legs were shaking when she separated them. Conner stepped up behind her and slipped his finger along her slit. Another gush of liquid filled her pussy.

He pulled his hand out from between her legs and then lifted the fingers to his mouth. She watched him in the mirror as he tasted her on his fingers. He made a low humming noise.

"You are always delicious." He caught her gaze in the mirror. "Wait here."

He left her, and she didn't move. She knew if he wanted her to, he would have told her. And God help her, that was a turn-on. The fact that she wanted to do it, that he would come back and be turned on by the sight, was so arousing. When he returned, he was naked, his erection easy for her to see. It curved up against his belly, and she couldn't take her gaze off it as she watched him in the mirror. She licked her lips. He chuckled and swatted her ass.

"You are a very bad girl, Jillian. Of course, now that I know you have a taste for my cock, I will definitely make sure you get that reward when you're good."

Then she noticed what he had in his hands. In one he held a vibrator, one of the toys he'd apparently gotten for her. The other, a package of lube.

"I want to fuck that ass tonight, but I want to make sure that you can handle it."

Without being aware of it at first, her spine stiffened. He chuckled. "This is for safety and for my peace of mind. Plus," he said as he turned the vibrator on, "you will love it, I am sure."

He stood behind her again, his cock against her ass, and she moved her hips. He closed his eyes and sighed.

"Naughty."

The way he said it made her think that he liked it. He liked it a lot. The idea that he would be turned on by that, then punish her, added another layer of need to her arousal.

He stepped back a second and slipped the vibe between her legs. He had it on the lowest level, but the tiny vibrations filtered through her body. The dampness in her pussy grew, and she knew she was probably dripping all over the toy as he turned up the vibrations.

"Open your eyes."

She did and watched him in the mirror. "Look down, at your pussy."

It took her a second, but she did it. He slipped the vibe between her pussy lips, and she sighed. He jacked up the speed, and she moaned.

"You wanna come, Jillian?"

"Yes."

"What?"

"Yes. Yes, Sir."

The moment she said it, his mouth moved over her neck and he whispered, "Come now, baby. Come for me."

She could do nothing else but obey. Her body was so in tune to his voice, she almost came on command. She shivered as her orgasm gathered then exploded through her system.

"Conner!" Her voice bounced off the walls of her bathroom.

"Goddamn, you're beautiful. Fuck."

He turned the vibe higher, and she came again, the orgasm almost bringing her to her knees.

By the time she was coming down from it, she almost fell. He pulled the vibe out and set it on the counter, easily taking her into his arms to carry her to the other room.

He laid her on the bed and kissed her forehead. "Be right back. Stay here."

He left her there, and she had time to catch her breath, but just barely. When Conner returned, he had the vibe and the plug in his hands. He set them on the mattress within reach, then he slid onto the bed beside her.

"How are you feeling, baby?"

God she liked the way he said it, the way he made it sound sexy. There wasn't anything derogatory or demeaning about it.

"Pretty damn good."

He smiled at that and leaned down for a kiss. It was almost sweet the way it started, a brushing of his lips against hers. But soon, his tongue slipped into her mouth, and she felt her body respond. She hadn't thought she could go another round, but the need he built up so easily in her was blossoming once again.

He kissed a path down her body, slipping his tongue into her belly button, then further down. Conner took his time as always, as if he were tasting the most wonderful of treats.

By the time he settled his mouth against her pussy, she was already starting to feel her arousal surge. Again and again, he plunged his tongue into her, building her back up, pushing her to that edge, but not enough to let go.

He pulled back a moment later and flipped her on her stomach. She let out a muffled shriek and a laugh.

"We are definitely going to have fun tonight."

She heard the way his voice deepened over the words, and it spoke to her. She had never had a man who could get her aroused by just speaking, but Conner could.

He leaned over her, and she knew he had picked up the lube.

"We'll take this slow, okay?"

She heard the concern threaded with need. It touched her that he would stop if she said no. He would not be happy, but he would do it.

"Okay."

She heard the rustling of a wrapper and knew he was putting on a condom. He slipped his fingers in first, and she realized that he had gotten some lube. The cool gel was the first thing she noticed. Then his finger eased in.

"Relax. Take a deep breath, let it out."

She did as ordered, and she felt his cock against her puckered hole. She tensed, and he leaned over.

"Remember, relax."

She nodded, and he eased in past the first ring. She'd had anal sex before, but not with a man who was so large. It took him a while to work his cock up her ass. By the time he did, she felt like she was going to explode. Slowly, he started to move. At first it hurt, but he reached between her legs and teased her clit. She tightened her ass in reaction, and he groaned.

"Fuck, yeah, that is good. So good," he said, smacking her ass with his free hand. The sting filtered over her, affecting both her holes, causing her to tighten on his cock in her ass again. He smacked her again, the sting shooting through her. Soon, the pain was forgotten. It mixed with pleasure, pushing her to another orgasm.

"Yeah, that's it baby, come for me. Now, I want you with me."

He pinched her clit hard, and she came then, her body bucking up against him as another orgasm filtered through her body.

"Yeah, that's it, fuck. Fuck!"

He thrust into her a couple of more times, and then he groaned her name, sinking into her ass and coming.

He fell over her and they collapsed on the bed. His breath was against her ear and she shivered.

"Are you okay?"

She nodded, but she could feel the tears again. Why did this man do this to her? He didn't really romance her, but he brought out a primal need in her she couldn't seem to deny.

It left her feeling raw and exposed.

With a sigh, he lifted himself up and then pulled out of her. He left to go to the bathroom, and she heard the water in the tub running.

For a moment, she wondered if he had just left her there to take a shower. But less than a minute later, he was back in the room. Without a word, he rolled her over, picked her up in his arms and carried her into the bathroom.

There were candles lit on the counter, and the tub was filling up with bubbles.

"You didn't have to do that, Conner." But it melted her heart just the same.

"You have to be careful. You need to soak. And since I saw you in the tub, I wanted to slip in there with you and just relax."

She looked at him and realized he was serious. That was a

big thing to get from Conner Dillon. She cleared the knot in her throat.

"I'd like that too."

He smiled as if she had offered him gold, and he stepped into the tub then set her on her feet. After they settled in, Jillian turned off the water and leaned back against Conner's chest.

"This is nice," he said, his voice filled with sleepy satisfaction.

"Yeah, it is."

And they stayed there, listening to the surf against the rocks, in the candlelight, and just enjoyed.

fourteen

Conner paced Jillian's small kitchen and tried to keep his irritation at bay. It hadn't been twenty-four hours, but he was ready for Devon to find something, anything, in his history.

"You're going to wear a hole in the floor, and I will add it to your tab at the end of your stay."

He turned around to scowl at her, and he stopped when he saw her. He was used to seeing her in her casual clothes. He wasn't prepared to see her in a dress. A definite fantasy of a dress at that.

It was blue-green, the same color as her eyes. The fabric was sheer and light. It draped her body, clinging to her full, rounded hips, and gave a hint of cleavage. The skirt clung to her legs, but when she walked, it seemed to float around her ankles. She was wearing some kind of strappy, high-heeled sandal, and to top it off, her toenails had been painted to match her dress.

"Conner?"

It took him a moment to realize he had been staring at her toes. He tore his attention away and finally looked up at her face. The barely-there makeup made her stunning, as did the light red lipstick she wore. She'd pulled her braids back and had something dangling from her ears.

"Conner?" she asked again.

He shook his head, trying to come to his senses. "Sorry, you just sort of stunned me."

Jillian gave him a dazzling smile. "Thank you. If it leaves you this stupid, I think I might put on a dress and heels more often."

Conner shook his head as he walked toward her. "Just the heels will do."

He slipped his hands around her waist and pulled her against him. She felt right against him, as if she was made for him.

"Oh, so you like the heels, do you?"

"Yeah. Cause it makes it a lot easier to do this."

He kissed her then, keeping his eyes open as he did it. She shivered, and he felt the familiar tug of need.

She pulled back from the kiss and narrowed her eyes. "Don't even think about it, buster."

"What?"

"I got all pretty, and you are taking me to a wedding. Got that?"

He frowned. "I think you got that wrong. I give the orders."

She grabbed him by the shirt and pulled him closer for a quick, loud kiss. "And I think if you want to keep giving those orders in the bedroom, you'll give me cake and champagne today. I hear Cynthia is the person in charge of the cake, and I do not miss a chance at getting something from that bakery."

He sighed. "The things I do for you."

She giggled, and he suddenly felt lighter. With her hand in

his, he walked her out the door, determined to enjoy the afternoon.

———

Jillian took a sip of some very good champagne and looked out over the crowd gathered for the reception. The ceremony had been intimate, filled with only the closest of friends and family. Probably because the chapel had been small. Here, though, the party was picking up steam. A unique gathering of cops, FBI agents—some who knew Conner—and Rough 'n Ready patrons mingled through the most beautiful room. She sighed, not able to avoid falling for the romance of the situation. She loved weddings and rarely got to attend them.

Maybe one day, Maura would get married. Then she could be in the wedding. She had never been a bridesmaid, and although she had heard horror stories about being an attendant, she thought it might be fun.

"How come a pretty lady like you is sitting all by her lonesome?"

Jillian set down her glass and looked up to find a deliciously cute Hawaiian man smiling down at her. It was genuine, as was the interest in his eyes. It was impossible not to return it with a smile of her own. His dark black hair was short, cut in a buzz with a bit of a flattop. Golden skin accentuated his blue eyes that tipped up a bit at the corners. She would gauge his age around twenty-one, and he had the body of a Greek god. Or, she thought with silent laughter, a Hawaiian god.

"I'm not by myself, but thanks for asking."

Without invitation, he slipped into the chair beside her.

"I don't think we've been introduced. My name is Danny Aiona."

"Of course we haven't been introduced. If we had, you would know I am here with a date."

His smile widened. "My name is Danny Aiona."

For a second, she said nothing, then the name clicked. She had met Evan Chambers beautiful wife just a few moments earlier, and her brother Kai.

"Oh, so you're the little brother?"

He laughed. "I'm not so sure you could call me that. I thought I saw you the other night at the club."

For a second, she couldn't think. She wasn't a woman who went for men a whole decade younger than she or were what she thought of as a pretty boy. But it was hard to resist his teasing smile and jovial manner.

"Club?" She couldn't think of the last time she had gone clubbing, then she remembered she had been at one club in the past week. "Oh, Rough 'n Ready? I was there for research."

He inched closer. In another man, she might have seen it as a threat, but with Danny, Jillian had an idea that it was all about seduction. A man his age knowing how to seduce a woman—and she was pretty sure he did—was a dangerous thing. "Do you need a subject for your research? I'd be willing to help."

Before she could say anything, a shadow loomed over them.

"Settle it down, son," Conner said from behind him. She peeked around Danny. Conner's voice might have been mild, but he didn't look very happy. And she knew from experience that Conner's easygoing voice was more dangerous than any man's yelling.

"Hey, old man. I was just having a conversation with this gorgeous woman."

She glanced at the younger man and realized he wasn't stupid. He winked at her, telling her he knew Conner was her date.

"That woman would be mine, and if you don't get up, I will gladly teach you how to behave when you are at a wedding."

Danny sighed and shook his head. "Change your mind, just let me know. May can give you my number or just come over to Paradise Cover Mondays, Wednesdays, or Fridays. I work there part time."

He stood and brushed by Conner without a comment. When Conner sat, she leaned over and gave him a kiss. "You know, he's just a kid."

Conner shook his head. "That was no kid. He's over the age of consent. And, as I heard him say, he saw you out the other night at the club. Means he has a membership."

"Probably free because he's Evan's brother-in-law."

He glanced at Danny with narrowed eyes then back at her. "You shouldn't have been leading him on."

She wanted to blast him and opened her mouth to do it, but it was then that she realized his behavior went beyond being irritated with her. He was jealous.

She had never been a woman who liked that emotion, from herself or others. But there was a kernel of truth to the feelings when you felt insecure about the one you were with. If he was worried about that, she knew he had more than just lustful feelings for her.

"I wasn't leading him on. He asked me what I was doing alone. I said I wasn't."

He looked away from her, but he leaned so close to her she could feel his breath feather over her ear. She shivered.

"You know damn well you're the most beautiful woman

here. You dress up like that, well, guys just can't help hitting on you."

"Are you telling me I can't be dressed like this? What should I wear?"

He apparently heard the warning in her voice. He looked at her.

"No, dammit, you look too pretty, and I like seeing you in a dress."

But he didn't sound too happy about it.

"You look cute too, Conner."

He grumbled something under his breath.

She couldn't stop the smile from curving her lips or leaning forward to brush her mouth against his cheek.

"How about we get some cake?"

He nodded but said nothing else as they walked to the table. A lot of the cake had been eaten, but of course that was to be expected since Cynthia's Bakery had done the work. A very pregnant woman with curly blonde hair was attending the table, and a very grumpy—not to mention sexy—black man stood beside her. She recognized Chris and Cynthia Dupree on sight. Both had added to what she referred to as her "hip" problem.

As Jillian and Conner approached the table, a toddler let out a screech and came running forward.

"You better come back here, you little rascal," a woman said, giggling as she ran after the little boy. When she grabbed him, the boy giggled himself as she hoisted him in the air and blew on his belly. The woman then settled him on her hip and walked to the table.

"Cynthia, I think Chris is right. Max and I came here for a reason—so you could rest."

"I have to hand out the cake. Then I am done."

The woman rolled her eyes and smiled over at them. Jillian was stunned. The woman was amazing, so small she was probably undervalued until you saw her face. She was gorgeous and the smile packed a punch.

"Max, go get your father. He needs to stop talking business with Evan and get over here." She set the little boy down who charged off to do her bidding. She noticed them and smiled. "Hi, my name is Anna. Want some cake?"

"Yes, I would love some cake."

She brushed back her long, curly brown hair and went to the table. She handed Jillian a plate that already had a fork on it. "Oh, look Cynthia, I handled that just fine."

Cynthia gave her a look filled with venom, but in the next instant, Jillian noticed something akin to pain in the woman's expression.

"You did a fantastic job, Anna, but I think you might want to go to the hospital," Jillian said.

"Really?" She smiled. "Why?"

"Cynthia's in labor."

For a second, no one reacted other than the mother to be. She gave Jillian a nasty look.

"What?" Anna asked.

"I was trying to make it through the reception," Cynthia said, her voice filled with pain.

"Lord, love a duck, Cynthia, we can't be having that," Anna said. "Maxwell, your ex-fiancée is having her baby. Help Chris because I am sure he's about to faint."

"Really, Anna, do you constantly have to remind me that I was once engaged to Max," Cynthia said as she waddled around the table. Her face was flush with excitement. Jillian noticed a man the size of a University of Georgia linebacker, with dark blond hair and a grim expression, make his way to the table and steady the dad to be.

"Whoa, son," Max said as he grabbed Chris, who almost pitched forward into the cake table in a dead faint. The southern she'd heard in Anna's voice was thicker in Max's. He easily steadied his friend, and then ordered, "Let's go."

Everyone apparently didn't have an issue listening to Maxwell. May Aiona came forward to take the little boy from Anna. Anna, for her part, was chattering nonstop as she helped Cynthia through the crowd.

"You know, you're allowed to say anything you want while you're in labor. I think I called Max an ass at least three times."

"Love, that was five times, along with referring to me as the sperm factory you were going to divorce when you were done with labor," Max commented good naturedly.

Cynthia laughed and Anna smiled. "It's all going to be okay."

A tall, athletic black woman who had the look of Chris Dupree rushed up behind them with a diaper bag. She was followed up by an older version of Danny Aiona.

"Well, hot damn, our first real Rough 'n Ready baby," Micah said as he walked up to them.

"It can't be the first one," Conner said as he slipped his arm around her waist.

"Not for the patrons, no, or even the employees. But we do have sort of a family we've gathered of friends. Dee and I will be the second in that group."

Jillian felt the unfamiliar feeling of envy at the pride she heard in Micah's voice. She might write erotic romance, but she had never planned on love or marriage. With her weird situation, she had thought it too hard to even attempt to find a man who understood. And she had been happy with that situation. Until now. Now, she had a feeling that until Conner left, and for many months after that, she would constantly wonder what it would be like to raise a rowdy bunch of kids with them.

Dee slipped into the circle, forcing Jillian to stop worrying about things that wouldn't happen. She smiled. "I cannot wait to get fat. I'm doing my best right now to gain weight."

She was shoveling cake into her mouth, and it was then that Jillian realized she never got a piece of cake.

"Oh, cake."

She walked around Micah and made a beeline for the table. Grabbing two plates, she turned and almost ran into Conner.

"Oh," she said as she handed him a plate.

"Are you going to tell me what's bothering you?"

She frowned up at him. "Nothing. I have cake, a good-looking man, and a pretty fantastic band to dance to."

"You looked kind of sad there for a moment."

"Oh." She took a bite of the cake and hummed at the taste of it. Pure, sugary decadence.

"Jillian?"

She glanced at Conner, saw the worry on his face and wanted to soothe it. Never in her life had she wanted to make someone she cared about so happy. What did that say about her?

"Nothing, I just get a little weepy at weddings. They're sweet."

He looked like he didn't believe her. "Really?"

"Yes." That much was true. "Starting a new life, all that crap. Makes me kind of happy and sad at the same time."

He snorted, but said nothing else as he ate his cake. Before she could finish hers, a hand wrapped around her wrist. She looked up and noticed it was Micah. "Come on, princess."

"What?" she asked.

"Bouquet time."

"Oh, God, no."

He nodded. "Yep."

"I have to eat my cake." But even as she said it, Conner was taking it away from her and smiling evilly. "You suck."

He shrugged as he dumped the rest of her cake on his plate and commenced eating it.

"I do not want to do this."

"Sucks to be you," as Micah pushed her forward into the fray.

She hated this. No matter what she did, she always ended up with the flowers. It sucked.

The band started playing a song, and she saw that Maria had picked her out of the crowd. She turned her back to the audience then tossed it directly in Jillian's area. Jillian tried to sidestep it, but the woman next to her dove for it, missing it. Instead, it bounced on the tips of her fingers and it hit Jillian in the chest. Instinctively, she grabbed for them.

Dammit.

She frowned down at them but didn't have a chance to do anything with them as she heard her name called out. Pictures. Great. She sighed as she walked to the stage. Better to get it over with quickly, just like ripping off a bandage.

Conner watched Jillian, trying not to laugh. "Looks like she's going to her execution."

Micah smiled. "Beware of the woman who doesn't want to get married."

Conner slanted him a look. "Yeah? Why's that?"

"You sometimes find yourself wanting to convince her otherwise."

Conner shook his head. "You really are getting to be like an old woman."

"You've been warned. I just wanted to let you know that Devon is still working on the list, but he's had a few hits that he's looking into."

Conner sobered. "Good. Anything promising?"

Micah shook his head. "In fact, he said most were nonviolent, so it isn't probably going to pan out."

The same familiar irritation he had been dealing with crawled down his spine. He knew that there was something they had to be missing. The fact that there seemed to be no lead was beyond troubling.

"I doubt we find anything, but I would feel better if all avenues were looked at," Conner said.

"Nothing from the police I take it?"

Conner shook his head as he watched Jillian walk back to him. "I'm hoping it was some freak but who knows. Even if it was random, I would rather find out and soon. These things rarely just go away."

Micah nodded. Both of them knew that more often than not, the problem would escalate. The fact that the bastard had been quiet for a few days meant nothing. Neither of them said anything to Jillian.

She shook the bouquet in disgust. "I cannot believe I caught another one. You saw that I didn't try to get it, right?"

He smiled. "How many have you caught?"

"Five."

"Five?"

She sighed. "Yeah. Every wedding I've been to since I turned eighteen. It's disturbing."

"I'm off to the hospital," Micah said as he leaned in for a kiss on her cheek. "You two have fun."

And with that, he left them alone. Conner looked at Jillian, who was still frowning down at the flowers.

"They're pretty."

She shrugged. "I'd rather not have them."

He laughed and grabbed her hand. For tonight, he would try to put everything else out of his mind and enjoy it. They had little time left together, and even though he knew they had to figure out what was going on, they needed tonight to be fun.

"Let's dance, love."

She gave him a smile and followed him, setting the bouquet down on a table on the way to the floor. In this, he could lose himself in her, the beauty of the music, and just how happy she made him.

"Where are we going today?" he asked as Jillian turned on to H-3.

He knew she had been itching to get out of the house for a couple of days, but he had been limiting trips out. They still had no leads. Everything Devon found was a dead end, and Jillian had been right about her living in Hawaii. Most people had no idea. Her family probably had some kind of idea, but they didn't know exactly where she lived, just that it was on an island and far away from them.

Every day she had grown more frustrated. This morning she had been snippy with him. It was the first time she had shown her artistic temperament. It would have been funny if he hadn't known part of the root of it was her fear. With each day, the tension had gotten worse.

So, when she had asked to go out and drive, he took pity on her. He knew he could protect her. While there had been some creepy pictures, there had been no physical threat to her yet. Sitting in the house wasn't going to solve anything and would make her resentful. Now they were racing down H-3 into Pearl City, and he had no idea what was planned. She had just told him to get his trunks on and they would have fun.

"I just thought we could change the scene up. I really like those little lagoons out in Kapolei. Thought we could just eat a picnic and enjoy a quiet day."

Since it sounded great to him, he wasn't going to complain. A light mist was starting to fall by the time she hit the last tunnel on H-3. When she drove out of it, the long descent started. He noticed she was driving faster than usual.

"Shouldn't you slow down?"

"Uh, I'm trying, but my brakes don't seem to be working." Her voice was threaded with enough fear that he knew she wasn't joking.

"What?"

She swallowed and drew in a shaky breath. "My brakes. They're not working."

Shit. Fear lanced through his blood as he started working on an idea for what they would do. The road was elevated, with no way to turn off until they got to the bottom. Anyone in their way would be hit. When he saw the safety run-off, he opened his mouth but she nodded before he could say anything.

"I see it, let's do it."

She headed onto the safety run-off and threw the car into neutral. The jeep jolted as it smacked against the poles. Glass crashed and Conner felt a few splinters bite into his cheek. He grabbed Jillian and tried to cover her as best as possible until they came to a shuddering halt. He rose and turned the car completely off.

Jillian was still bent over, and his fear morphed into outright panic. He didn't want to grab her in case she was injured.

"Are you okay?" He asked.

Slowly she rose, pieces of glass falling off her braids as she looked at him, then the mess around them. She nodded, but she said nothing.

"Jillian."

She looked at him then, and he realized she was in shock. Her body shivered, and her eyes were dilated.

He started to look for his phone but he heard the sirens in the distance. He got out of the jeep and carefully made his way around to her side. Pulling open the door, he tugged her out.

The police showed up and came running forward. "What happened? Are you two hurt?"

Conner looked down at Jillian and saw some of the cuts on her face. "Yeah, we're going to need to be patched up. Both of us."

She was plastered against him as if she were trying to burrow somewhere safe. Anger spiked through him as he thought about what could have happened. Jillian was a good driver, but she could have easily been on Kam Highway on one of the sharp turns or could have crashed into someone else. He had no doubt in his mind that this was on purpose.

He was going to kill someone and fucking enjoy it while he did it.

"Sir, can you tell me what happened?"

"The brakes went out on the jeep."

The officer nodded and put in a call for medical. Conner tightened his arms around Jillian and thanked God that nothing had happened to her.

fifteen

Jillian sunk down below the bubbles hoping that the heated bath water would get rid of some of the aches from the wreck. Who would have known that a simple crash would make her feel as if she had been beaten up? She would have never known she could end up with so many bruises from an accident. And in the oddest places. Her ass even hurt.

"You look like you're feeling a little better."

She looked up at Conner and felt the tears well up in her eyes again.

"Baby, don't," he said, walking forward. Just like a few days before, he sat on the tub, but there was no seduction in his gaze now. She recognized the worry she had seen in his eyes from the moment they had gotten out of the jeep.

"Sorry," she said, then took a deep breath. "I just don't feel that great right now. My emotions are all over the place."

He nodded.

"It doesn't seem to be affecting you."

He took her hand and threaded his fingers through hers.

"No. I am ready to kill someone right now. If I knew who it was, I would go beat the bastard to death."

She would have laughed it off if he hadn't said it with a dead certainty that had a chill going down her spine.

"I made some soup. Doc said that it was important for you to keep your blood sugar normal tonight."

She nodded, but he didn't look happy. "Come on."

She stood as he helped her out of the tub. He grabbed one of her towels and wrapped her in it. Then, he picked her up and took her into the bedroom. He had a pair of panties and a shirt laying out for her. He set her on her feet. "I'm going to go get the soup. I'll be right back."

"I can eat in the kitchen."

"I know you can, but I want to do this for you."

He said it in a way that had her chest hurting. Lord, the man was adorable.

"Get dressed and get into bed."

She nodded and waited until he left to pull on the panties and shirt. She was under the covers by the time he returned with a bed tray that had a bowl of soup on it. He set it on the mattress in front of her. "I just brought you some water because I wasn't sure what you would need."

"Water's fine."

She took a sip of the soup. It was just canned chicken noodle soup, but it felt so good to eat something warm. He turned on the TV, stripped down to his boxers and pulled off his polo shirt. When he turned, she saw the bruising on his back.

"How did that happen?"

He looked over his shoulder. "I guess it happened in the wreck. It's not too bad."

She sighed. "I'm so sorry, Conner. I never meant for you to be hurt."

She felt the tears well up in her eyes again, and she couldn't stop them this time. He picked up the tray, set it on the floor and joined her on the bed. Instead of complaining or telling her she was being silly, he pulled her into his arms and held her close.

"It isn't your fault."

"It is. Some crazy hates me and wants to kill me. For whatever reason. And you got hurt in the process."

She felt like a fool, crying all over him, but she couldn't seem to stop. He held her like that for she didn't know how long. She hated not being in control. To think that someone hated her enough to kill her was sickening. When she had calmed down, she pulled back, embarrassed.

"I'm sorry."

"Did I say I wanted an apology?"

He sounded mad. When she looked at him, she realized that he was pretty mad at her. "I'm—"

"I swear if you say you're sorry, I am going to take you across my lap and give you a spanking you won't forget."

For a second, she didn't say anything. Then she snorted.

His expression softened as he cupped her cheek. "I'm mad at myself."

She frowned. "Why?"

"I should have taken this more seriously. I should have let Rome do an actual report. Without him here, we are going to have to handle it through HPD. I'm okay with that, but I put you at risk by not acting on it."

Of course he would feel responsible. "It isn't your fault."

"I'm trained at this sort of thing."

She sighed. "I forgot you're perfect too."

She said it with enough humor that his lips twitched like she'd hoped.

"Yeah, I am that."

She sobered. The enormity of the situation could not be ignored. "What are we going to do?"

"For tonight, we have the protection of the HPD. Tomorrow, I'll secure the house more. I've had a talk with Adam and Mick. They are going to help with security until we get a handle on just what the hell is going on. But right now, what I want to do is lay here, hold you, and watch TV."

He was sincere. That she would never doubt. And it seemed so simple, but she knew it was more than that. He was there for her, without question. Since her folks had died, she had never had anyone stand up for her, offer her a shoulder to cry on. In this, he offered her something else no other person had. Comfort. If she wasn't careful, she would start crying again.

She swallowed the tears and sniffed. "I think that sounds like a great idea."

Conner held out his arms, and she snuggled against him, putting her head on his chest. As they lay there, she gave up running or even pretending that she was just having an affair. She was knee-deep in love with Conner, and there was no going back now.

Three days later, Conner was ready to come out of his skin. Nothing. They had no leads at all. There was something they missed, he was sure of it, but just like before, he couldn't even fathom what it was. He knew that he was missing something. There had been no indication of any other issues.

"So, the brake line was cut?" Micah asked. Conner nodded but said nothing else. He needed to talk about it with someone. Jillian was working, and he didn't want to talk it over any more with her. She was beyond irritated with him, the situation. She understood she had to stay home or only go out with him to be safe. It didn't make her very happy.

"You said the last time you used her jeep was a week ago?"

He nodded as he stood to pace the small kitchen. "Dammit, this is really starting to piss me off. Seriously. In any given crime, I can always find a motive. Something to give the person away. I know there has only been two incidents, but it seems like something should have popped up by now. Even if it didn't tell us right off, I would give my left nut for a lead."

"I agree. Every avenue seems to have been traveled. Which means it's probably a stalker. A very skilled stalker."

Conner didn't even want to think of it. Just contemplating a stalker made him itchy. Plus, it would have to be someone with amazing detecting skills, and that would make the bastard dangerous. It could be a crazed fan, someone who was infatuated with her. She'd had no emails or physical mail to indicate it, but that didn't mean anything. With someone like that, a motive didn't matter. Their main existence was all about the subject of their infatuation. It made no sense, and there was no way to know exactly where they would go with it.

"Devon could have missed something," he said, but even he heard the defeat in his voice.

"I know nothing about that."

He glanced over at Micah and found him grinning.

"What?" he asked.

Micah shrugged. "Hey, if you get arrested, I am claiming I knew nothing of it. But, no, he is sure he has been very thorough. There's nothing there that he can find."

"The thought that someone just picked her out on a street, it creeps me out."

"And if you go with my instincts, I say not right. It feels more personal than someone who just saw her on the street. This is someone who knows her. Someone who really doesn't like her, but they know her well enough to find her."

Conner stopped pacing and looked out the window. He rolled his shoulders, trying to ease the knots in his muscles. "Everyone she has had contact with has been checked out. Even that asshole who hit on her that night at Rough 'n Ready."

Micah frowned. "Who?"

"That Aussie from the Big Island."

"Oh, St John? I could have told you it wasn't him."

It had annoyed Conner that he hadn't been allowed to pull the son of a bitch in to question just for the hell of it. Conner was sure the cowboy was hiding something behind all that sickening charm. And he still wanted to break his arms.

"I found out he was back on the Big Island before any of the incidents started to happen. I even checked out Evan's brother-in-law."

"Kai's married."

Conner stopped pacing and sat down in the chair across from Micah. "First of all, you know that doesn't rule him out, but I'm talking about Danny. The younger one. He hit on her at the wedding."

Micah's lips twitched. "Let me guess, you weren't happy?"

"Not really. He knew she was there with a date, but apparently it didn't stop him from sitting at our table and trying to pick her up. When he tried to cut in while we were dancing, I wasn't thrilled either."

"I guess that was later, after most of us had gone to the hospital for Cynthia?" Micah asked.

Just the memory aggravated Conner all over again. It wasn't that he didn't trust Jillian. He knew when she said she was with him she would never cheat. The woman had a true sense of honor. But he didn't like the feeling of jealousy Danny Aiona had brought out in him. It was juvenile. Even knowing that, it had taken more than just a little of his control to keep from starting a fight.

Worse, he knew what bugged him more than anything about Aiona. In a few weeks, Conner would be gone. He had read the message in the younger man's expression. Just thinking about another man touching Jillian had Conner grinding his teeth.

"I keep telling that boy to be careful," Micah said. "He has a taste for older women, especially black women."

"He saw her at the club when she was there a couple of weeks ago. He mentioned it."

Micah nodded. "Believe it or not, he's a Dom, and he is in hot demand with the women, especially the older subs. They know he likes them at least ten years older."

"Well, it's not him." And that chapped his hide. Conner would have loved to have a reason to beat the crap out of St John or Danny. Even now he was balling his fingers up into a fist. Conner counted back from ten mentally and relaxed his fingers.

"And you've checked out everyone?"

He nodded. "Yeah. I have no idea what the fuck to do now."

Micah leaned back in his chair and crossed his ankles. "I think you just need to be careful."

The frustration of the last few days boiled over into anger. He knew Micah was only trying to help, but dammit, he had to yell at someone. "Be careful? Someone tried to kill her."

Micah studied him for a moment. "Listen, man, I know what you're going through, believe me."

He blew out a breath and gained back some control of his emotions. Yelling at Micah wasn't going to help. It made him feel better, but it wasted time. "I know."

"I had to fly to Vegas thinking Devon had abducted her to hand her over to their bastard of a father. Over six hours on the plane before I got there."

Thinking back to that time, he remembered seeing Dee's brother for the first time in person. "Did Devon ever forgive you for that broken nose you gave him?"

"I guess so since I'm giving him a niece or nephew to spoil. You know those Italians, they love family."

He snorted then sobered. "I'll go back over the list. The police are now involved, of course. Without Carino here, they put someone else on the case, but they are hitting dead ends."

"And you're here. That will ward off some of the worry, I'm sure. Anyone who is thinking about bothering her here will be hesitant. Especially with those two bikers who are hanging around next door. They looked at me sideways when I came up." He glanced out the window then back to Conner. "I take it you put in some cameras?"

"Yeah." Conner was still kicking his ass for not taking it more seriously at first. Of course, the brakes could have happened anywhere, but it still might have helped. They had punctured holes in the lines, and they had been leaking for a long time. "I just can't figure out who would want her dead."

"It's because you're too close to her because you love her."

That stopped him, and he frowned at Micah. He had been through this with other friends who were married. They always thought every relationship he had was serious.

"I didn't say I was in love."

Micah shook his head. "Bra, you don't have to say you're in love. It's written all over your face."

"You're talking shit."

"Tell me, would you normally sleep with your sister's friend? Or perhaps you always feel this murderous when men talk to women you date?"

Shit. No. He rarely got jealous, and from the very first, he had been over Jillian.

When he said nothing, Micah continued. "I doubt you would have taken her to bed with your entanglements if you weren't in love with her, man. Hell, you're practically living together."

"We aren't living together, and we aren't in love."

"Why don't you tell us exactly how you feel, Conner?"

Both of them looked over. Jillian was leaning against the doorjamb with her arms crossed.

"And I think this is where I come up with something witty to say and leave," Micah said as he rose.

He walked toward Jillian, giving her a kiss on the cheek. He said something to her that Conner couldn't hear, then he walked out. The door shut with an almost quiet click.

She didn't say anything. He was accustomed to quiet. He could outlast the worst suspects and reduce them to tears. Now, though, he felt the need to fill the space.

"You weren't supposed to hear that."

Conner inwardly cringed. Now he sounded like even more of an ass.

Her eyebrows shot up. "Apparently."

"Listen, Jillian--"

She held up her hand to stop him. She had no expression, and he wished she did. Even if she were pissed, he would rather deal with that. She was one of the most expressive women he had ever met, but now she looked solemn.

"You don't have to explain. I never asked for anything. I don't expect anything."

It was what he would have told himself if she'd thrown a fit. Now, though, it made him feel small, so he couldn't help but speak the truth. "But you should."

The smile she gave him had his heart turning over in his chest.

"I stopped giving a damn about doing what I should the day I punched my date to the deb ball and broke his nose. I pretty much do what I want now."

He shook his head. "You should expect more."

"I don't expect. My expectations are not what someone else might want. I live life like I want to and expecting things from other people would conflict with that."

"What do you want?" he asked, almost afraid to hear the answer.

She cocked her head. "Nothing more than for you to accept that I love you."

She turned and left him alone in the kitchen. For a moment, his brain would just not function. She had stunned him once again. From the first, she had been honest to a fault, and there was no artifice in her.

Conner shook his head. He wasn't looking for this, for her, for what she was doing to him. He had an ordered life. His business was exactly where he wanted it. But why was he working so hard? He had more money than he knew what to do with, and he just kept worrying about making more. And where did it get him? Maura and he were set for life. They didn't need anything else. But he had worked hard, and harder still. It was then that it hit him. He had been missing something else in his life. And until now, he hadn't realized it wasn't more money or power.

It was Jillian. It was sappy to think that way—that the one thing he was missing was love, but it was true.

He followed Jillian to the back of the house and found her on the computer in her office. It was a crazy space filled with everything that would drive him insane. Books were stacked haphazardly on the bookcase. She had pictures on every surface, some personal, some professional, but they littered every available table. Framed posters decorated the walls.

Two weeks ago, he barely knew the woman. He knew *about* her. Her family, her background, but he didn't know her. Now he did. He knew that she was honest and hard working, loyal to a fault, and so giving that it stunned him. He knew that she lived a simple life and more importantly, he knew what she sounded like in the morning when she first woke up.

"Are you going to keep staring at me?"

"If I want to."

He couldn't see her expression but he knew she was smiling.

"Come with me."

She stopped typing. "Is that an order?"

He thought about it. For once, he wasn't sure. He knew if he ordered her to do it, she would. He didn't want that. "A request."

She glanced at him, and he held out his hand. She didn't hesitate. When she slipped her hand into his, he felt as if something shifted inside him. If she had refused, he wouldn't have pushed it. At least he hoped so. Right now, he wasn't sure what his emotions would cause him to do. He was always so sure of his next actions, but since the first, he had been off-kilter with Jillian. If he could, he would blame it on his situation.

She rose from the chair, and he led her back to the bedroom. There was part of him that needed just this. The last few days had been horrible, and he just needed her there. In that bed. The need to dominate was still there, but now he needed something else, something more. He wanted to show her how he felt without words. That meant more to him.

He pulled her into his arms when they were in the bedroom, and his entire body reacted. The frenzied need she always inspired in him was there, but something else was there, also, something the he was afraid to address. If he were honest, it was as if he'd found the place to just be him.

Jillian lifted her face at the same time he was bending his head to kiss her. The soft, sweet kiss soon transformed. His blood roared with a hunger that almost unmanned him. He wanted to pull her on the bed, just take her. But he wanted to love her, to let her know just how much he needed her.

He pulled off her tank top and sighed when he slipped his hand over her breasts. Her head fell back as she moaned. Conner licked his lips before he leaned down and took her nipple into his mouth. She moaned again, and the Dom in him didn't want to be ignored. He bit back the need, or tried too.

Jillian must have sensed it in him, as she always did.

"Conner."

He lifted his head, and she took his face in her hands before kissing him. The kiss was hot and wet, and he felt it all the way to the soles of his feet.

When she pulled back, her eyes were heavy lidded, her lust easy to see.

"Take me to bed."

The command had his body reacting before he could do anything about it. Need crawled through him, and he tried one last time to keep it controlled.

"I wanted to be gentle," he said.

"Do what you want. I'm yours."

She whispered the words against his mouth. It was like a balm to his soul.

"Are you sure?" he asked.

She pulled back and cocked her head as she studied him. "Are you scared?"

Yes.

He was. The woman scared him more than anything in his life. Serial killers had been easier to handle than this one woman. She had the ability to see into his soul, and dammit, she apparently liked what she saw there. But, he said none of this.

Instead, he leaned down, keeping his eyes open while he did it. When he pulled back, he slipped her board shorts down her legs and sighed. She hardly ever wore panties with them and today was no exception. The tiny palm tree charm dangled from her belly button, shimmering against her skin. He was easily becoming addicted to seeing all those tats and piercings.

He knew if he ordered her, she would do anything. She would allow him to control everything, and that was part of his personality. But as a seasoned Dom, he also understood other needs. And now, he needed this. He needed to show her with his actions how he felt.

He picked her up and laid her on the bed, then joined her there. Covering her body with his, he took his time, tasting her skin, loving the way her body moved against his mouth. By the time he reached her sex, she was already moaning his name and moving against him.

The flavor of her slammed through him. He grazed her clit with his teeth and enjoyed the way she shivered. But that was not enough. He wanted more.

He pulled away and reached for the condom. After he had it on, he pulled her up on top of him. She looked down at him with the setting sun slipping through the cracks in the blinds behind her, bringing out the gold that rimmed her eyes.

"Take me in," he ordered.

Her lips curved, and she lifted up off him, taking his cock in one hand and then sinking down on him. They both let out a sigh when she sunk all the way down on his cock.

Then she started to move. He couldn't tear his gaze away from her. Gorgeous, her body seemingly made for him. Soon, though, he was ready. He wanted to come, and he wanted her there with him. He reached up, teasing her clit, and she gasped. He felt the first shimmer of her orgasm as her muscles flexed tighter on his shaft, and he could no longer hold back.

His orgasm shattered him. He thrust up into her one more time and felt his body drain as she came again.

She collapsed on him, their breathing the only sound in the room. Jillian pulled herself up and leaned over him.

"I do love you, Conner."

He opened his mouth, but she kissed him.

"Don't. I know you care, and that's enough for me."

And if he told her what was in his heart, she would never

believe him. Instead, he pulled her close and accepted that one day they would both deal with it.

Jillian watched the waves crash against the rocks below. A winter storm had hit, and it was definitely a bitch. Normally, she would enjoy the snapping of electricity in the air and the chaos it created. It always seemed to fuel her creativity. Since there weren't that many of these kinds of storms in Hawaii, she always relished when one hit the island.

Now, though, it was too close to what she was feeling inside.

She stood and walked around, trying to ease the tension threading in her veins. Since the night before, she couldn't seem to calm herself. She lived her life in a certain order. People thought she was some kind of weird bohemian without a care in the world, but she had things that weighed heavily on her mind.

Her entire family despised her, but they depended on her to keep everything tight. They came to her with every worry, and she had to deal with their mistakes and downfalls. She had a wealth of readers who wanted the next book now. She loved them, but the pressure wasn't easy to deal with. Not with everything else she had going on.

Falling in love was something she hadn't planned and wasn't ready to deal with at the moment.

Conner hadn't said anything about it after they made love, or in the three days since then. She hadn't been expecting it, but she had felt oddly depressed that he hadn't. She usually kept her feelings hidden. The only person she was so open with was Maura, but how did she call a woman and tell her she loved her brother but the butthead wasn't being nice about it?

Oh, he had been nice in his way, she thought. The love-making had been beyond what she had experienced before, even with him. Yes, she had felt cherished, loved in a way she never thought possible. She had also felt as if it had taken her to another level—as if he had claimed her. Since then, it had been the same. She'd had no real thought other than what pleasure he would give her. Every time they were making love, she had given him complete and utter control over her, and she didn't regret it.

Before this, she would have thought it enough for her. Commitment wasn't something she liked because it tied her to something for too long. She was truthful the other night. She didn't expect an answering declaration from him—but she had hoped for something from him. For once in her life, the words were really important.

"I'm going in to talk to Micah about this. Mick is downstairs."

She glanced over her shoulder. It was surprising that he was even thinking of leaving her alone. She had told him she had work to do. Not that she thought she would be able to write with her emotions so unsettled.

"So you trust him now?" she asked.

"I told you I did. Plus, even if I didn't ask, he and Alex see this as their job now. They want nothing to happen to you."

She shrugged and picked up her mug of tea. Usually, her Zen tea calmed her, but it wasn't doing her any good today. She was unsettled in some way, as if she was waiting for the other shoe to drop.

"You need to be careful."

She felt silly after saying it. Something told her that she was saying it more for herself than for him.

He walked over to her and slipped his arms around her waist then pulled her back against him. He dropped his chin on top of her head.

"After we figure this out, why don't you come to Miami for a visit?"

She guessed it was an offering, something that she should be happy with right now. And normally, she would be. But now she wanted something beyond a vacation fling or even an affair.

That annoyed her more than anything else.

"I'll see if I can work it into the schedule."

She sensed he wasn't happy with that answer, but he said nothing. That was the problem. They weren't connected enough to be truthful. She had upset him with her declaration, but she wouldn't hide it. She loved him, and if she had to deal with it, so did he.

"If I had my way, I'd order you to Miami right now."

She slipped away from him. "Order me?"

He shook his head. "I'd rather have you in my house, locked up safe."

"I'm safe. People will see anyone who shows up, and well, Mick can beat the shit out of them. It's been almost a week since the brakes, and with this weather, there won't be anyone coming to this side of the island. I'll be okay. Go on, talk to Micah."

He looked unsure of himself, and there was a part of her that really enjoyed that. He sighed, gave her a brief kiss that had her heart turning over and her blood churning. He set his forehead against hers.

"I'll be back soon."

With another quick kiss, he walked out of the room. She watched as he stepped out into her yard where Mick was standing.

She opened the window. "Hey, be careful. A storm like this could get you stuck on the other side of the island."

He looked up at her and gave her that heart-stopping smile of his. "Don't worry about me, love. I'll make it back to you no matter what."

sixteen

"So one of those neighbors is protecting her?" Micah asked.

Conner nodded, but he didn't stop moving. He couldn't. He had never felt so fucking useless in his life.

"I probably should have stayed."

But he was a coward. He had left because he couldn't deal with the emotions. It wasn't like him at all, since he was used to facing all his trouble head on. With Jillian, he didn't seem to be able to handle anything.

"She's safe. I have a feeling even a gorilla wouldn't be able to get past the biker. Truth is, your stalker could be gone."

He shrugged as he looked at the dark video screens. It was the middle of the day so the club wasn't open. "HPD said the same thing."

Conner didn't believe it, couldn't. It was bothering him in a way that it had when Dee had been attacked years earlier. His gut feelings were usually right. He started pacing again.

"Will you quit walking around? You're making my head hurt. Shit," Micah said from behind his desk. "It's bad enough I have to put up with Devon right now."

"Hey, I'll leave you with Dee and you can handle the weepies all by yourself," Devon said.

Micah made a face, and Conner couldn't help but laugh. "So the hormones are going crazy?"

Micah sighed. "I swear if I look at her wrong, she starts crying. It is either that or sex. She has turned into a maniac."

Devon groaned and made a face. "Oh, lord, please, don't talk about sex and my sister while I am in the room."

Conner smiled. "I have to agree with you there. I think of her as a little sister."

"But you never saw Jillian that way?" Micah asked.

He thought back to when he met her and knew that he hadn't. "I wasn't interested in her then. Hell, the only thing I had on my mind was my sister and the job. I checked her and that insane family out, and knew that Maura had a good roommate. And I was right. But I don't think I ever put her in the category of sister."

"That's good because that would be gross," Devon commented.

"She's a few years older than your sister?" Micah asked.

"Yeah, Maura went to school so much earlier than people her own age. And Jillian, she seemed kind of worldly."

"Like she had been around?" Devon asked.

"Excuse my brother-in-law."

Conner shook his head. "That's okay, the CIA is known for being uncouth."

Devon stuck up his middle finger.

"And to answer the question, no. It was more that she was wary of men in general, of everyone." Conner blew out a breath. "With her family, it is understandable."

"She was raised by her grandmother?" Micah asked.

He nodded and settled in the chair in front of Micah's desk. "Her white grandmother who reminded her every day that she was lucky to be there. She really had no options."

"If so, it's odd what she did with the will," Devon commented.

He glanced at Devon. "What do you mean?"

"She's in charge."

"What do you mean?" he asked. "In charge of what?"

Micah apparently read his mood. "Please explain to Dillon what you mean or he might beat you up."

The younger man snorted. "He could try, but we all know that the FBI is bad at killing, and we always win in a fist fight. What I mean is that she is in charge of the money. Every major expense goes through her. Nothing is done in Bentley Industries without her approval."

"She said that she had to be there when they voted for things. Like she was part of the board."

Something niggled at the back of his mind, and the hair on the back of his neck tickled. He stood and walked over to where Devon sat with his computer, and Micah joined them.

"Show me."

Devon pulled up the court documents.

"It took me a while to find them. There were a lot of cases on it, filings. The cousins, aunts, and uncles fought the will. They said that Jillian had tricked her grandmother, that she had used something as leverage to get all the money. But your woman has a lot of money, from her father and from her writing, so she didn't really need this stuff. And who would? From what I found, your woman's family is insane. I mean crazy beyond just being an old southern family with some loose nuts. They sue each other at the drop of a hat."

"And the will held up without an issue?" Micah asked. Conner couldn't form a question because he was still taking it all in.

"Yeah. Partly because Jillian has a lot of money, as I said. Even before the writing, her father and mother made sure there was money for her. The court dismissed every one of the cases. It helped that the grandmother had a former Georgia Supreme Court Justice write the will."

"You found all that in there?" Conner asked.

"Well, you asked me to be thorough. She is in charge of a corporation that makes billions of dollars."

He was still trying to take it in. He knew she had money, knew that she was definitely beyond comfortable. She had kept it all to herself, not wanting to let him know that part of her life. He had known there were things she hadn't told him, but knowing the truth of it hurt more than he expected. "And she lives in a little house and acts like none of it matters."

"Because it doesn't," Micah said.

"If it didn't, she would have told me. She never mentioned this. And if they know this, they would know where she was."

"I can't tell you that, but what I can tell you is that some cousin of hers is on the island."

"Who?"

"Brent Edwards. And he isn't happy with her. From the communication that I could read—"

"Wait. What laws did you break with my computer?" Micah asked.

The younger man shrugged. "Just a few. Nothing big. And nothing the FBI could find."

Conner's frustration boiled over into anger. "Just stop the arguing and tell me where he's staying,"

Devon glanced at Micah then back to him. "In Ko'Olina."

"He has no money but he's staying there?" Micah asked.

"You know how rich people are. They somehow figure out a way to do things like that. Always."

Conner knew he spoke from the experience of growing up with a mob father. And he was probably right. There was always a chance Brent would just disappear when he was done here, and the hotel would have to fight him for the money.

"Let's go," Conner said.

"And you need to call Jillian. She needs to know that nut is here," Micah said.

He called her number as they headed out of the door of Rough 'n Ready. The wind just about blew him over as they stepped onto the sidewalk next to the club. There were dark clouds gathering. She picked up after a couple of rings.

"Sorry, I was moving my grill in. The wind is just insane and the rain is hitting us now. How is it over there?"

"Fine. Why didn't you tell me that you are in charge of Bentley Industries?"

She didn't say anything, and he didn't blame her. He had planned on asking her calmly after they sorted everything out with her cousin. Instead, it had come out as an accusation. He should have waited, but until that moment, he hadn't realized that her not telling him had hurt so much.

When she finally answered, her voice was very measured, as if trying to make sure that she didn't reveal too much. "I'm not really in charge. I just handle the money that goes to the family. I sit on the board, but I only go in for the annual meeting or if there is an emergency."

He stopped and Micah and Devon gave him some privacy.

It was hard to talk on the phone with the wind blowing like it was, but he knew he needed to try and at least apologize. "Sorry, I didn't mean to be a bastard about it, but your cousin is here in the islands."

"Brent? He's harmless."

It rankled that she wasn't taking it seriously. "Why is he here then?"

She sighed. "He has a temper, but believe me, it's only when he drinks, and he wouldn't fly over the ocean to deal with me. That isn't his style. That would take a lot of concentration, and that's something Brent's never had."

"Still, we're going out to Ko'Olina to talk to him."

"We?"

"Micah and Devon are coming with me."

She sighed again, and this time it sounded more like relief. "Okay you have a local."

"Think I can't handle myself?" he asked.

"No, but Micah will know that the weather can look like paradise one minute and be a disaster the next. Locals know better how to handle it, and they know better ways to get around the island. Plus, there is a chance that you might have to wait the storm out over there.

"I'm not going to allow that. We're going to take care of this, then I will be back."

He didn't want to say it, but something was really feeling wrong to him. Other than his usual worries, that gut feeling that told him something bad was about to happen was in full force. It had never let him down before, but Conner hoped that this one time it would.

"Call me when you get there."

He waited for her to say she loved him, but she didn't. She hadn't said it since that night when she had first told him.

"I will. Bye, Jillian."

"Bye. Oh, and Conner?"

"What?"

She hesitated. "I love you." She hung up before he could respond, but it didn't lessen the affect. Warmth spread through his chest as he felt his lips curve. Damn, if the woman didn't make him happy. Micah beeped the horn on his car, and Conner jogged over to get in. As soon as this was straightened out, Jillian and he were going to have a talk.

He was just starting to realize that he didn't want to contemplate living without her. She was just going to have to accept it.

The ride out to Ko'Olina was as aggravating as the entire issue had been. It was long, and the slow pace of Hawaii was no longer enjoyable. He had to get there and see that bastard of a cousin. Once he did, he would know that he could control the situation.

By the time they drove past Paradise Cove, Conner was counting the number of Brent's fingers he would break. Micah didn't get the car in park before Conner was out and striding to the door of the resort. Devon and Micah caught up to him when he started toward the front desk.

"Don't, I have the room number," Devon said.

"And?" he asked as he started toward the elevator.

Devon rattled off the number. He was about to take the stairs when the doors opened. They waited while people got off, then he strode into the car. The boiling anger he'd felt was now exploding. The minute the doors opened, he bolted, looking for the room. He banged on the door with his fist.

"What?"

"Brent Edwards?" he bellowed.

The man on the other side of the door hesitated. "Who wants to know?"

Conner opened his mouth to answer, but Devon stopped him.

"This is Devon Ross with the Honolulu PD. There is an emergency with your mother."

"His mother?" Conner whispered.

Devon shrugged. "From what I read, he is a real mama's boy."

"My mother?" The locks flipped and the door opened. The man he saw standing on the other side of the threshold was a big brute, at least six foot and extra. He had to weigh close to two hundred and fifty pounds—most of it muscle.

"What's wrong with my mother?" he asked.

Conner didn't answer. All the rage he'd barely controlled took over. He balled up his fist and hit the bastard in the nose.

"Fucking hell," Brent yelled as he covered his face with his hands. Blood came seeping from between his fingers. Before Brent could respond, Conner hit him in the stomach. But what he hadn't expected was another man, even bigger than Brent, coming at him. He tackled him with such force, Conner and he fell onto the ground.

By the time they pulled them apart, Conner had gotten a few hits in, but not without receiving a few himself. He was feeling a little dizzy by the time he stood.

"What the hell is this about?" Brent asked. He was now holding a towel to his nose.

"Jillian."

Brent shook his head as if he were trying to clear it. "My cousin Jillian?"

Conner rolled his shoulders. "Don't play stupid. You came here, you sent her threatening mail, played with her brakes."

He glanced at his friend, then back at him. "When?"

"Now."

"When?" he asked again.

"Okay, I'll play along. This past week."

"There is no way," Brent said. "We've been here this week."

"Yes, and that's why I want to know what the fuck your game is."

"Let me explain," his friend said. "My name is Justin. I'm his husband. We've been on our honeymoon."

For a second, no one said anything. "You're married?" Conner asked.

"Yep, we went to DC and did the deed, then we flew out here," Brent said. "We've been here most of the time, other than a quick trip to the luau down the road last night."

Conner couldn't wrap his head around the situation. He was so sure it was her cousin, and now he might have an alibi. He had to be lying. "I know that the attacks have to do with your family."

"Dude, I seriously didn't have any idea where Jillian lived. We stayed out of each other's way."

Conner opened his mouth to ask another question, but Justin stepped in. "Before we answer any more questions, you have to tell us who the hell you are."

"My name is Conner Dillon, and I'm staying over at Jillian's for the month. She's a family friend."

"Is that what they call it?" Micah murmured as he stepped forward. "My name is Micah Ross. Conner hasn't explained it properly, so let me."

Micah outlined the two incidents quickly. "There was no indication of a reader fixated on her and there was no one in Conner's FBI past who was following him. It all goes back to the family."

"But your mother calls for money constantly for you," Devon said.

Everyone turned to look at him, and he winced. It was then that Conner realized he might not want these people to know who he was.

"I've had access to the records. Your mother has asked Jillian numerous times for money over the last few months. When she was turned down, your mother filed papers trying to remove Jillian as trustee."

Brent sighed and sat down at one of the chairs. "My mother is insane. From the time she was a kid, she resented Jillian's mother. She was always brighter, smarter, and my grandmother adored her. When she died, Grandmother was devastated. I was young, but I remember. My mother, she was thrilled."

A cold chill sunk into Conner. "Thrilled."

He nodded. "She was finally the oldest. She thought she would control everything. But as much as I think my grandmother was a bitch, she was a smart one."

"Your grandmother?"

He nodded. "She knew that the one person who would keep us all in check would be Jillian. I promise that I haven't had her go to my cousin for money in two years."

"And you didn't come here to find Jillian?"

"I've been a little busy. I do know Mom lost some money."

His husband snorted. "Please. She didn't lose the money. She went gambling. The woman has a gambling habit that she passed on to her son. Don't forget she has the drug habit, too." He looked at Conner. "Oxycontin."

Brent smiled. "Mom had always been able to keep it under control. Then Dad left. He was never really there to begin with, but he left, and Mom hated dealing with the embarrassment of having her husband marrying a woman younger than her son. Since then, Mom has gotten worse, but I don't live in Atlanta anymore. I moved to Seattle to be with Justin and help him run his shop."

"Shop?" Micah asked.

"We customize motorcycles."

"Can you think of anyone who would have it out for her in the family? You all seem to have a motive, but do you know someone who thinks she is beneath you."

"Most of them do. I never did. Truthfully, by the time I was old enough to know what was going on, she had gone to college. Then she was completely gone."

Justin shook his head. "Babe, tell them the truth. Your mother has the most to gain."

"What?" Conner asked as the chill that had worried him was now sending waves of fear through him.

"His mother. She will control everything if Jillian is killed. And God help the rest of the family at that point."

Before he could say anything, his phone went off. The number was from Atlanta.

"Dillon, here," Conner said.

There was a pause on the other side of the phone. "Yes, sir, I was trying to get ahold of Ms. Sawyer. She isn't answering, so I called her contact, which is a Maura Dillon."

"Yes, that's my sister."

"So I surmised. You really should tell your sister when things are bad because she is none to happy with you. She apparently didn't know about the threats to Ms. Sawyer."

He was impatient as the worry that had plagued his gut earlier today grew. "What did you need?"

"I wanted to let you know that it has come to my attention that her Aunt Blanche knows where she lives. I found out that someone from my firm told her several months ago."

"When?"

"About four months ago. I am very sorry for this."

"Do you know where she is?"

"Ms. Sawyer? I thought she was there in Hawaii."

He almost threw his phone against the wall. "No. Jesus, Blanche."

The man cleared his throat. "That is the problem. No one can locate her."

Panic now threaded through his blood as he thought of the ramifications. "Thank you."

He hung up as the man continued to talk. He punched Jillian's number but all he got was a busy signal.

"Busy. I can't get ahold of her."

"The other side of the island is getting hit hard now. The lines will be down probably," Micah said.

"We have to go."

"What does this have to do with my mother?" Brent asked.

"She apparently knows Jillian lives over here. To top it off, she seems to have disappeared off the face of the earth."

"Shit," Justin said. "She's probably the one."

That had Conner stopping. "What makes you say that?"

"She was furious when Brent came out. She tried to beat him with a poker. As it is, it took seventeen stitches. And that isn't the first time."

Brent sighed. "When she is mad, especially when she's drinking, she can be bad."

Now, the panic was quickly becoming replaced with terror. It was screaming through him as he tried to keep himself in check. "Fuck. Let's go."

"Wait, I can go with you," Brent offered.

Conner already had the door open. "I don't have time."

"It might be smart, depending on if she is there, Conner. Brent might get her to calm down," Micah said.

"Okay, but I'm not waiting." He grabbed a piece of paper off the desk and wrote down the address. "Use the GPS and meet us there."

He rushed through the door then down to the stairwell. He wasn't going to bother with the elevator. Conner wanted to believe that he was overreacting, but as he heard Micah running behind him, he knew he wasn't. The something that had been missing now clicked into place. There had always been something kind of personal about the pictures, something that told him it was a person who knew her well.

He pushed those worries aside as he ran through the lobby. He didn't even stop when he saw the rain. It looked like a fucking monsoon was hitting, but he didn't pay attention.

All that mattered was getting back to Jillian. He tried once more to call and got the same busy signal.

"It's the storm," Micah said. "We don't get many, but when we do, they can cause a lot of problems."

Conner nodded but said nothing as he tried to get ahold of

Mick. Busy. He was pushing the buttons to call Jillian again as Micah pulled out onto Farrington Highway.

"We'll get there, don't worry," Micah said.

Conner prayed that he was right because any other option wasn't acceptable.

seventeen

Jillian splashed water on her face, trying to wake herself up. Now that the storm had hit, she was starting to get kind of sleepy. It was dreary out, and the rain was lashing against the windows. There was an odd kind of rhythm to it. It made Jillian think of getting her E-reader and cuddling in bed with it. She wished Conner was there to snuggle with her.

Jillian opened the bathroom door when all the lights went out.

"Mick?" she called out.

Silence greeted her. Not the pleasant silence that she sometimes relished. This was odd, almost unsettling. It could be because of the storm, but something else wasn't right. Jillian looked out the window and noticed that the house next door had light. That wasn't right. They were on the same line, so if she had lost power because of the storm, they should have too. A flash of lightening brightened the room. She noticed a pair of shoes on the other side of the kitchenette table. She knew then it was Mick. Jillian hurried over to him. He was lying on the floor, his head bleeding and his eyes closed. She leaned down, but a chilling voice stopped her.

"Hello, Jillian," Aunt Blanche said.

Jillian slowly turned in the direction of the voice. She couldn't see much without the lights, but what she did see scared the ever-living crap out of her.

Blanche was a woman who always dressed properly, without a hair out of place, and her clothes were always from the best stores. Now, though, her hair was a mess, her face dirty, and her clothes looked as if she had been sleeping in a ditch. Even in the dim light, Jillian could see the crazed look in her aunt's blue eyes.

"Surprised?"

Jillian tried to inch closer to Mick. A flash of lightening brightened the room, and Jillian saw the gun in her hand.

"I wouldn't do that if I were you."

Jillian stilled, her panic tickling the back of her throat. She swallowed it. She needed to be smart to get out of here and save Mick.

"It was you."

Blanche smiled. It was all teeth and almost as lethal as the weapon she held. "Yes. Always. I am always the one who has to get things done."

Jillian's heart was beating so hard she was afraid she might pass out. She fought the tears that burned the back of her eyes. Showing Blanche her fear would be a mistake—one that her aunt would use.

"How long have you known where I lived?" Jillian asked. She was proud of the fact that her voice wavered only slightly.

"Four months." She shrugged. "Not too hard to bribe someone for the information."

"Why?"

"Why?" she asked in a parody of Jillian's voice. "My whole life I spent trying to please that bitch. I did everything right. I went to the right school, pledged to the sorority my mother wanted me to, and I even married a man I loathed to please that bitch."

"Grandmother."

"Jesus, I was glad when she finally died. Truth be told, if she hadn't died then, I was ready to do the job."

"You didn't kill her." Jillian knew that was a fact.

"No, the cancer did that. Thank God. She deserved it, you know. She spent my life making me miserable. Until your slut of a mother ran off with your father. Oh, my, that pissed the old bitch off, and then, everything was wonderful. It was as if your mother was no longer alive."

"Then she wasn't."

"She was going to change her will. You know that if Mother had died then, I was going to get everything. Then you were born. I'm sure that you don't know that your bitch of a grandmother kept the announcement of your birth in her bedside table. As if she cherished you over my son."

A lump formed in Jillian's throat. "Did she? It was hard to tell."

"She was still mad at your mother. For some reason, she thought she had let your mother down. She thought she had been too easy on her—which was true. Then she was dead, and instead of just letting you go into the foster system, she brought you home. As if you had a place with us."

Jillian shook her head. "You're mistaken. She was worried how it would look."

Her aunt snorted. She had heard the sound many times, but

now it sounded odd. It had a strange quality to it. Jillian had to swallow the nervous laugh that threatened to escape. She had to keep her aunt talking.

"You stupid woman. She adored you. Do you know how many times I heard her tell that story about you hitting Gerald Swanson and breaking his nose at the deb ball? Hundreds."

"She had a funny way of showing it."

"It was because she thought she babied your mother too much, and she did. She made her life so easy while she ignored me. I could have been just as successful as your mother, if I had that kind of support."

"My mother did what she did on her own. She accomplished all that because of who she was. She worked hard."

She snorted again. "No! It was Mother. I never had the support that she had."

Jillian inched closer. If she got close enough, she might be able to get the gun away from her aunt.

"And then what? You had Grandmother to yourself for ten years, and you didn't do much more than marry a loser who ran off with your maid."

"You bitch!" She swung out at her and clipped Jillian across the jaw with the gun. Jillian saw stars as she stumbled back and fell on the floor.

"He died in a wreck."

Jillian shook her head, trying to clear her vision. "While running away with the maid."

"You have a mouth like your mother. I took care of her, just like I will take care of you."

For a second, her world stopped. A chill slipped down her spine, one that had her blood freezing. "Mother? Father?"

"I know how to work on a car. Just a little nick in the brake line and it looks like an accident."

Slowly, the knowledge of what her aunt said registered with Jillian. Rage exploded. Jillian jumped to her feet. The only thought that she had was killing her aunt.

"You fucking bitch," she yelled as she tackled Blanche.

They toppled over onto the floor, Jillian landing on top of her. Before her aunt could react, Jillian grabbed her arms. She continued to struggle, though, and the gun went off. Jillian felt the sharp bite then burn of the bullet. She rose and stepped back. Her head started to spin, the room turning into a merry-go-round. There was banging on the door, but she didn't react. The rush was gone, and now she felt as if she were moving in slow motion. Her aunt had risen and was pointing the gun at her, but Conner crashed in through the door. It took him only a moment to assess the situation and tackled her aunt from behind. The gun skidded across the floor. Blanche screamed in anger or pain, or maybe both. Jillian couldn't figure it out. The edges of her vision were starting to dim.

The multitude of voices filling the room hurt her. She looked around, but she couldn't seem to figure out who was there. Heck, she thought she heard Brent's voice. Then she was falling, but before she hit the floor, someone had ahold of her and picked her up.

"Baby, stay with me," Conner said, his voice hard to hear.

"I shot her, I shot her!" her aunt screamed.

"Get that crazy bitch out of here or I will make sure to shoot her."

Her vision was dimming. Bile rose in her throat, but she swallowed it back. She tried to lift her arm but it didn't seem to want to work.

"Conner."

"Babe, be quiet. Rest."

She heard the desperation in his voice, but she didn't understand it. Again she tried to raise her hand, but it just didn't move.

"How is she?" Micah asked.

"She's lost some blood. When is the fucking ambulance going to get here?"

"Mick," she said.

"Don't worry. He's okay," Conner assured her.

"I love you, Conner."

"Dammit, Jillian don't..."

It was the last thing she heard as her world faded to black.

"What did the doctor say?" Micah asked as Conner returned.

"She's going to be fine. The loss of blood wasn't as bad as I thought it was."

Micah slapped him on the shoulder as Conner looked around for Devon. "What happened to your brother-in-law?"

"Devon has a habit of making himself scarce when the police arrive."

Conner nodded as he sat in one of the chairs that lined the hallway. "You might as well go home. It'll take a while to get her into her own room. With the storm, they're short staffed, and of course, there have been more accidents than normal."

Micah ignored him and sat in the chair next to his. "You need to get some scrubs."

Conner looked down and saw the blood on his shirt. Jillian's blood.

"What the fuck did she think she was doing attacking her aunt?"

"Saving her life and Mick's."

He glanced at Micah, who was leaning back against the wall with his eyes closed.

"How's he doing?"

"Fine. Being a pain in the ass according to Adam. He had ten stitches, but you know what a head wound is like. Mild concussion. They are keeping him overnight for observation."

"And Blanche?"

"The police took her into custody. She'll go before a judge in the morning."

He nodded and opened his mouth, but someone was yelling his name

He turned his head and saw Maura running down the hall, her hair flying behind her as she practically jumped into his arms.

He caught her close as Zeke came running behind her. "She wouldn't sit still, and I told her she had to pay for the trip over on the jet."

"How did you get here so fast?"

"We were in LA on the job. We got the phone call hours ago. When Maura couldn't get ahold of you or Jillian, she got us over here."

He glanced at the clock, trying to figure out how many hours they had been in the ER, but he had lost track of the time.

Maura hugged him tighter. "I keep finding you in hospitals. I don't like that."

He heard the tears in her voice. He gave her an extra squeeze. "This time it isn't my fault."

Maura pulled back and looked up at him, her green eyes bright with unshed tears. "How's Jillian?"

"She's okay. They're stitching her up right now."

"Just now. What's taking so long?"

He shook his head at his sister's indignant tone. "You missed the storm that hit. It was horrific. It took us forever to get here, and then there were some life-threatening situations."

Maura settled her hands on her hips. "I don't care. Jillian is special."

Micah chuckled behind him. "Like brother, like sister."

Conner shook his head again and found his first smile. He had screamed the same thing when they had arrived hours earlier.

"Mr. Dillon," a nurse said from behind them. "You can go in to see her, but only you. The doctor's orders."

Maura didn't look happy.

"I'll be right back. I'm sure you could use some food." He looked at Micah, who nodded.

"Come on, I know this hospital well. I spent a few days here a couple of years ago."

Maura hesitated, but Zeke sent Conner an understanding look and grabbed her hand.

"Come on, love. You can't do anything here, and I am sure that Jillian will want to see Conner first."

She shook her head. "Give us a minute."

The other two men waited for Conner's nod.

"You're in love."

She didn't ask. She didn't have to. They might be years apart in age, but they were closer than a lot of siblings.

"Yeah."

She smiled. "I'm happy."

"I'm not."

She laughed. "And?"

"What?"

She rolled her eyes. "We could use a Hawaiian office, ya know?"

"Are you trying to get rid of me?"

She shook her head as she sobered. "What I want is that the two people I love most in the world be happy."

He sighed. "We'll see."

She kissed him. "Call if you need me."

She hurried off, and he shook his head. It seemed that in a way, their roles had reversed. He followed the nurse back. Jillian was in a smaller room inside the ER and blessedly alone.

She looked so...quiet. That was something he wasn't accustomed to with her. She was always so full of life, so ready for any and all adventure. Seeing her like this was unnerving.

"Are you going to keep standing there staring at me?" she asked, her voice weak.

His lips curved and a sense of rightness filled him. "If I feel like it."

He walked forward and slipped his fingers beneath her palm.

"I thought I heard Maura yelling your name. I must be out of it."

He lifted her hand and kissed it. "No, she's here with Zeke."

She sighed as she opened her eyes slightly. "Mick?"

"Fine. He's got a concussion but he's fine. He'll be home tomorrow."

Her eyes slid shut, and her breathing evened. He didn't want to give up her hand, so he hooked the leg of the chair with his foot and pulled it over. He sat there, looking at her. Less than a month ago, he had never thought to settle down, never thought he would be able to have a woman understand him. Jillian did. She might not see what she did for him, but she never questioned his nature. She either let him be, or pulled him out into life. She gave herself to him in bed without a thought.

Whether she had figured it out yet or not, she was his. She would just have to deal with it.

eighteen

Several days later, Jillian was sitting on the back lanai, unhappy with the situation. The sun was shining, the trades were cool, and she had friends and family to make her happy. But she wasn't.

"I want to go in the water."

"The doctor said no," Conner said.

She looked out at Zeke and Maura playing in the surf. Resentment filled her. She felt as if she was coming out of her skin, and she didn't know what to do about it. She was snarling at everyone, but Conner in particular.

"Then get my laptop."

"No."

The need to yell at him almost choked her, but before she could say anything, the sliding door opened and her cousin stepped out.

"Hey, cuz."

She couldn't stop the smile he brought about. Brent and she had never been close before, but the one thing that had come out of the mess her aunt had created was that she and

Brent had become closer. And that would piss her aunt off, Jillian thought with a silent laugh.

"Hey, yourself. How are you doing?"

He bent down and gave her a kiss on the cheek as if it was something so ordinary. To her, it made her feel...weird and kind of wonderful at the same time. She hadn't had close family since her parents had died, and it was kind of cool.

"Fine."

"Can you tell Conner that I should be able to go swimming or write?"

Brent looked at Conner, then shook his head. "I think I would rather not. Your boyfriend has a mean punch."

She looked at Conner, who continued to read over his iPad as if none of them were there.

"At least let me answer email." Oh, God, she sounded whiney, and she hated it.

"No."

His easy answer, along with the quiet control he had shown since she'd gotten out of the hospital, was starting to piss her off. She didn't know why, but it made her want to scream.

"Quit being a pain in the ass."

He looked at her, then at her cousin. Without a word, Conner stood and went into the house, closing the door behind him.

"What was that?" she asked.

Brent sat down in the chair Conner had just vacated. "Give the guy a break. He's been through a lot."

"Him? I was shot, and I almost died."

"First of all, you didn't almost die. Yes, I know my mother shot you. But, that man had the living hell scared out of him.

233

You didn't see him pounding on the door, and you didn't see him at the hospital."

"He felt guilty."

"Maybe a little."

She sighed. "So, where's Justin?"

"He's off on the bike. I wanted to see you."

She smiled at that. Even with the aggravation she felt, she was really starting to like Brent. "He's really pretty, you know. I wish you had told me you were gay."

"I didn't tell anyone but my mother."

"Who freaked."

"Yeah, I was worried what you would do when you found out."

She snorted. "Please, I knew."

His eyes widened, and he shook his head. "You did not."

"I was back for break from college. It lasted two days because Grandmother went on one her of her tirades. I saw you making out with Javier."

He rolled his eyes as his face turned red. "I can't believe you spied on me."

"Spied on you?" she asked. "You were going at in the garage."

"That man did have a way with machines," he said with a sigh.

"And that still gets to you."

"I guess so. I guess it is the whole sharing an interest thing. I loved working on engines. My mother also freaked when I told her what I wanted to do. She insisted that I go into banking." He rolled his eyes, and his dimples appeared when he grinned at her. "Can you imagine me doing that?"

She looked at the young man and realized for the first time

just how different he looked. His dark hair was longer than normal, and he had a goatee. The cut-off shorts and T-shirt could have been blamed on the vacation, but she bet it was a way of life now.

"No, no I can't."

"So, when are you and Mr. Right Cross in there going to get married?"

She shrugged. "He's going back to the mainland. This was just a fling."

There was a beat of silence. "Uh, no it isn't."

"What are you talking about?"

"That man almost felled me with a punch. I'm not that small, but there was a lot of rage behind that hit."

She shrugged that off. "Conner has a real sense of right and wrong."

"There was more to it than that, I promise. If Justin hadn't been there, I think Conner might have beaten me unconscious."

Why did that make her so happy? "Really?"

"Yeah, what has he said about staying?"

She sighed. "I'm too afraid to ask."

"You? Jillian Sawyer, the girl who fought my mother for a gun, who punched her date in the nose, and told Grandmother that she was an uptight, selfish bitch? You're afraid?"

She pulled her legs up and wrapped her one good arm around them. The fear that had been riding her since she'd gotten out of the hospital now hit her full force. Since they'd been home, Conner had done nothing more than kiss her. "What if he tells me he's leaving? That would just kill me."

He leaned forward and brushed her braids back from her face. "It wouldn't kill you."

"I've never been in love before. I don't know how to handle it. What if he tells me it was just for fun?"

"Then Justin and I will beat the shit out of him."

She laughed even as she felt a little tear escape. "Okay."

She looked into his blue eyes, the expression serious.

"Don't take a chance and let him disappear from your life. You deserve to be happy. Plus, since Justin and I aren't into raising our own kids, we want some more nieces and nephews to spoil. Especially me, because my side of the family kind of sucks except for you."

She laughed.

"Go get him, Jillian."

She leaned forward. "You're kind of cool, cuz."

She gave him a kiss on the cheek and went in search of Conner. She didn't find him in her area of the house, but when she looked outside, his rental car was still parked beside her cousin's bike. Footsteps sounded upstairs, so she knew he was there.

With each step up the staircase, her heard sunk a little. The courage her cousin had spoken of now seemed to be dissolving. She reached the landing and took a deep breath before knocking.

"Come in."

She pushed the door open. He wasn't in the living area, but she heard him in the bedroom. Following the noise, she found him there, his bags half full of his things. Her heart sank.

"You're packing."

He didn't look up from his task. "Yes."

"I didn't know you planned on..." She swallowed the words. Just saying that he was leaving would hurt too much. Tears clogged her throat.

"Well, it's the only solution."

She felt her heart tear, but she would be damned if she would let him see it. "Fine."

"You're going to need a new bed."

He zipped up his case and set it beside the dresser and looked at her for the first time. He didn't look happy. In fact, he looked furious. She glanced at the bed behind him.

"What did you do to it?"

"Nothing, but if you think I'm going to sleep on a fucking double bed, you're crazy."

For a second, she didn't compute what he said. She blinked, trying to compute the words in her brain. "What?"

"I said I hate doubles. I'm a big man. And for the things I want to do to you, we need a bigger bed. Hell, we need a bigger bedroom. We're going to have to renovate the house."

She shook her head, trying to figure out what he was saying. "Wait, back up. Who said you were staying here? And who the hell said you were staying in my bed?"

"You did."

"I did not."

"You did the night you told me you loved me. All bets were off then."

She would have settled her hands on her hips if her arm wasn't in a sling. The nerve of the man. "So that means you have the right to move in with me?"

"Well I love you too, you idiot, so yeah, it does. It means we get married and have kids," he shouted at her.

Silence followed the storm, and she stared at him. He looked so unhappy, she almost laughed. "You love me?"

"Yes, although I have no idea why. Jesus, woman, I put up with a lot, but this has got to take the cake."

She snorted.

"And don't laugh."

Something tickled her throat. Instead of a laugh, though, a sob rose to the surface, catching them both off guard.

"Oh, baby, don't," he said as he fell to his knees in front of her and wrapped his arms around her waist. He rested his head against her stomach. "I'm sorry. I've been an ass."

Jillian tried to stop the tears, but she couldn't. Her eyes were overflowing with them. She leaned down and kissed the top of his head. Conner lifted his face to look at her.

"I think I knew from the beginning I cared for you, but it wasn't until you told me you loved me that I realized how much I wanted that. Wanted you...forever."

She leaned down and kissed his forehead. "Can you tell me why you haven't touched me since I got out of the hospital?"

He rose then and pulled her into his embrace, being careful of her injured arm. "I was afraid if I touched you that I would expect too much. After almost losing you, the man in me wanted to claim you all over again. It's stupid, but with your injury, we have to be careful."

She looked up at him. "We can be careful."

He opened his mouth, but she rose up and brushed her lips over his.

"I promise to be gentle."

He laughed at that. "Really?"

"Yeah."

She stepped away and tugged her shirt over her head slipping it easily over her arm. Then, she smiled at him. "Come on."

He pushed his suitcase onto the floor and laid her down on

the bed. He lay beside her, resting his head on his hand. "I really love you, Jillian."

"I love you, too, Conner."

He brushed her braids back from her face as he leaned down to kiss her. He worked his way down, licking and nipping at her flesh as he pulled her pants off her body. Settled between her legs, he looked up at her.

"There is one thing I can expect from my sub right now."

"Really?" she asked, her voice husky even to her own ears.

"You don't get to come unless I give you permission," he said as he leaned his mouth closer to her pussy. He teased her then, his tongue driving her out of her mind until she was begging for relief. When he finally took her, they rode the crest together as they gave themselves over to the ecstasy.

epilogue

Jillian drew in a deep breath and settled back against the couch cushions. A slight breeze blew the curtains, bringing in a touch of salt and freshness to the living area. They'd been hit with a massive winter storm, which had battered the windward side of Oahu for a couple of hours. Thankfully, she and Conner had a generator, so everything kept running even after the storm knocked down a few power lines. Now, all she had to do was wait for him to make it home.

She sipped her ginger tea and sighed. Her stomach had been giving her problems for a couple weeks, and she found out this morning why. When she took the test, she almost called Maura, but she'd been in those meetings that Conner had to handle today. Granted, it was by teleconference, but Jillian would not interrupt their business. Also, Maura wouldn't be able to keep it a secret. And even if she managed to keep her mouth shut, Conner would freak out, thinking something was wrong.

Her phone buzzed.

Conner: *Almost home.*

He didn't go into the office that much anymore, but today had been important. Dillon Security just signed a big contract, and Conner felt he needed to be there. She had been convinced that he would spend more time in the office once they settled into married life, but he did most of his work from the home office. With her pregnancy, he would become even more insistent that they buy an apartment close to the Dillon Security office. It made sense, but she wasn't about to tell him that.

Her phone buzzed again.

Mick: *I think we might float away.*

She rolled her eyes. Mick and Adam were out in Maui on a quick two-night getaway. They were in the thick of the storms hitting right now, but Maui seemed to be getting more rain and flooding.

Adam: *Dramatic much?*

Mick: *I told you we shouldn't plan a trip in the winter. Every time we do, we end up stuck inside.*

She smiled.

Jillian: *Are you guys sitting in the hotel room group texting?*

Adam: *Maybe.*

Mick: *Yes.*

They texted at the same time. Her smile faded. She was going to miss them when they moved into their new house. They were looking for a place to buy. She knew they would probably be no more than fifteen minutes away, and they still did contract work for Conner. And yes, they wouldn't be too far from her, and they did contract work for Conner, but it was still change. Usually, she loved change. Thrived on it, actually. But right now, her life was changing.

She settled her hand against her still-flat stomach. In eight and half months, they would have another little person in their lives. It was hard to believe all the changes in her life since Conner was forced to come to Hawaii for a vacation.

Adam: *You would think you would devise something to do since we're stuck inside a room all day.*

Mick: *Bye Jillian.*

She laughed out loud. Those guys never change. She always thought things got stale the longer you were in a relationship. Mick and Adam had taught her that wasn't always the case. And she knew that things couldn't be better for Conner and her. In fact, he'd woke her up that morning to make love to her before his meetings.

She heard the rumble of an engine, and she looked outside again. Conner was home. As she watched him unfold his considerable length from the car, her entire body heated. It didn't matter how long they had been together; butterflies erupted each time she saw her husband.

He made his way up the stairs to their main living space. He had been right; they needed to expand, and they had. The house was now twice its size when he had vacationed with her. She rose from the couch as the door opened up. After setting down her mug, she walked into his open arms.

"I'm glad you're finally home," she said, her words muffled in his shirt.

He wrapped his arms around her, and she breathed in his scent. Sandalwood and rain. It was a heady combination. Jillian wasn't usually this clingy, but the last few days had been difficult for her. Her emotions were all over the place. She was just going to blame her hormones.

"Let's settle down, and you can tell me about your day," he said, stepping back and taking her hand to lead her to his favorite chair. After sitting down, he pulled her down on his lap.

"So, did you get any writing done today?"

As Jillian complained about her lack of focus, Conner played with one of her braids. It had been a pretty good day until the storm had hit. He blamed himself for getting stuck in Honolulu. He couldn't control the weather, but he could pay attention to the freaking forecast.

"So, when the storm hit, I gave up. It was too hard to concentrate."

These last few weeks, she'd been distracted. In fact, she had been all over the place. Conner's normally organized wife was scatterbrained. He would worry if he didn't know why she'd had problems staying on task. He wondered when she was finally going to tell him she was pregnant.

"I think you might be right about getting an apartment in Honolulu if we can swing it."

He was surprised by that. She hadn't wanted to spend the money. For growing up with money, Jillian was frugal. So, he'd put a down payment on a three-bedroom in town. He figured they could sell it or use it for Dillon Security if she didn't like it.

"Is that a fact?"

She nodded, then her eyes filled with tears. Alarm lit through Conner. "Baby, are you okay?"

"I'm just sorry I fought you on it. You could have been hurt coming home. You would have been home much earlier if we had an apartment."

That didn't bother him. He'd lived in Miami before Honolulu, so he was accustomed to dealing with storms. His worry had been Jillian. She was an independent, kick-ass woman who could take care of herself. However, he still didn't like her being at the house alone in a weather emergency. They had a generator, but power wasn't what he worried about. Their home was surrounded by trees, and he'd rather not be here for a downed tree.

And now that she was pregnant, he didn't like the idea of her over here alone. There were times when the ocean water came up and over the road, effectively cutting off parts of the island.

Why hadn't she told him she was pregnant?

"About that. I found an apartment in town, just off Ala Moana."

He knew she liked that area and always said that if she were to live in town, she would pick the location. The apartment had amazing views of the ocean and the mountains. He hadn't wanted to wait because the building rarely had any apartments for sale.

"Is that a fact?" she asked as she played with the buttons on his shirt before squirming on his lap. He had been half hard before, but his cock hardened, his blood heated. She looked up at him through her lashes. The smirk she sent him was full of sensual promise. This woman...she would always get to him. There was no doubt in his mind that he'd react the same way even in his eighties. That sensuality entwined with his love for her was a head combo.

"Yeah."

Need threaded his voice. Jillian slipped off his lap and then turned to straddle him. There was no denying his aroused state.

"Jillian, I think you have something to tell me."

She moved her hips, pressing her sweet cunt harder against him. His fingers spasmed on her hips. The knowing curve of her mouth had another wave of heat coursing through his blood, which was all headed south. Fuck, he was amazed if he could remember his name at this point.

She set her hands on the back of the couch and leaned forward.

"You do?" Her husky voice, the breath against his ear...what had they been talking about. Oh, right. She was pregnant and hadn't told him yet.

"Yes," he said, then he nibbled on her earlobe. "Don't make me order it out of you."

She snorted. They still played, but they were comfortable with their roles, each knowing exactly where they stood with each other.

He knew he wouldn't last long in this situation. They had been together for years, and she knew exactly what buttons to push. Instead, he slipped his hands under her ass and lifted her up as he stood. She wrapped her legs around him as he strode into their bedroom. Once he set her down on the bed, he tugged down her board shorts, finding her wonderfully naked beneath them.

"Now, will you tell me what's going on?"

She smiled, and it was then that she realized he knew. He smacked her pussy. Her eyes dilated.

"Make me."

Conner smiled, his entire body going hot.

"It will be my pleasure," he said as he pulled her to the edge of the bed. Dropping to his knees, he placed a hand on each of her thighs. Her pussy was wet, practically gushing with need for him. He licked his lips.

Glancing up, Conner noticed she still hadn't removed her shirt.

"Take that shirt off."

She didn't hesitate, throwing it on the floor somewhere behind him.

"Now...about this secret."

Her throaty laugh sent joy careening through him. Lowering his mouth to her pussy, he set about torturing her until she told him the news.

Conner just hoped he lasted long enough.

rough fantasy

What starts out as a simple fantasy among friends becomes an overwhelming need that none of them can deny.

Buy the book!

Maura Dillon has always been someone who lived life on her own terms. From the time she was in college, she knew she had different needs than most of her friends. Still, she never thought she would find herself torn between two very sexy men, or that they would want to add her to their relationship.

Zeke Bryant and Rory McAllister have known each other most of their lives. Their casual relationship has spanned a decade, but now that they are living together, things are on a whole other level. Add in their mutual attraction for Maura and things are getting out of hand.

Rory understands their desires and suggests their week in Hawaii be more than just a vacation. No rules, no limits, no regrets. But as their nights are filled with unimaginable erotic pleasure, there is someone lurking in the shadows. Someone who wants revenge, and will stop at nothing to succeed.

»Warning: This book contains the following: Two sexy men who are hot for each other and the heroine, more Hawaiian scenery, a Dom who thinks he can control everything, two lovers who know he can't, and scenes that will push even Harmless Addicts over the edge.

love free books?

USA TODAY BESTSELLING AUTHOR

MELISSA
SCHROEDER

Hey, there. I want to encourage you to sign up for my VIP newsletter. I stuff it with all kinds of fun things, including sneak peeks at upcoming books, insights into what I am working on at the moment, and newsletter only contests!

Best of all, you can get a free book for joining. Check out The Sweet Shoppe Collection today. It's three stories about magical chocolate or you can grab Only For Him!

If you aren't interested in all the goodies I have in my newsletter, you can sign up for my RSS Feed. It is a just the facts kind of email that will tell you about new releases, preorder, and appearances.

about the author

From an early age, USA Today Best-selling author Melissa loved to read. When she discovered the romance genre, she started to listen to the voices in her head. After years of following her AF Major husband around, she is happy to be settled in Northern Virginia surrounded by horses, wineries, and many, many Wegmans.

Keep up with Mel, her releases, and her appearances by subscribing to her NEWSLETTER. If you want to keep up with cover reveals, new behind the scene info on her writing, and when new excerpts are posted, follow her MelissaSchroeder.net News News. Or you can do both! They are low traffic, so you will not get tons of emails.

Check out all her other books, family trees and other info at her website!
If you would want contact Mel, email her at: melissa@melissaschroeder.net

instagram.com/melschro

amazon.com/author/melissa_schroeder

facebook.com/MelissaSchroederfanpage

bookbub.com/authors/melissa-schroeder

goodreads.com/Melissa_Schroeder

tiktok.com/@melissawritesromance